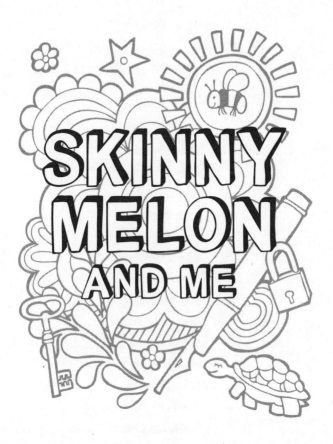

Also by Jean Ure

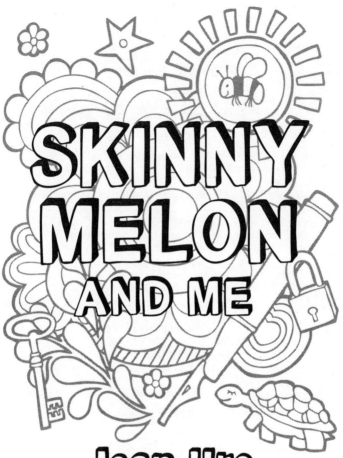

SKINNY MELON AND ME

Jean Ure

Illustrated by
the equally masterful pens of
Chris Fisher and Peter Bailey

HarperCollins *Children's Books*

First published in Great Britain by Collins 1996
This edition published by HarperCollins Children's Books 2011

HarperCollins Children's Books is a division of HarperCollinsPublishers Ltd,
77-85 Fulham Palace Road, Hammersmith, London W6 8JB

The HarperCollins Children's Books website address is
www.harpercollins.co.uk

Jean Ure's website address is
www.jeanure.com

1

SKINNY MELON AND ME
Text copyright © Jean Ure 1996
Illustrations copyright © Peter Bailey 1996, Chris Fisher 1996

The author asserts the moral right to be identified as the author of this work.

ISBN-13 978-0-00-742485-6

Printed and bound in England by
Clays Ltd, St Ives plc

Mixed Sources
Product group from well-managed
forests and other controlled sources
www.fsc.org Cert no. SW-COC-1806
© 1996 Forest Stewardship Council

FSC

Monday

Skinny Melon and me have decided: we are going to keep diaries.

Skinny is going to start hers on Saturday when she has bought a special book to do it in. She says it is no use doing it in an ordinary pocket diary with spaces for each day as there will be times when we feel like writing a great deal and other times when we may not want to write anything at all, except perhaps what we had to eat for dinner. I agree with her but feel inspired to start immediately and so cannot wait to buy a special book but am using an old writing block with wide lines (I can't stand narrow ones).

I think when a person is writing a diary they ought to introduce themselves in case it is unearthed in a hundred years' time and nobody would know who has written it, so I will say straight away that this is the diary of me, Cherry Louise Waterton, aged eleven years and two months, and I am writing for posterity, in other words *the future*.

To begin with I suppose I must put down some facts, such as, for instance, that I am medium tall and neither fat nor thin but somewhere in between, have short brown hair and a fringe, and a face which is chubbyish (I think I have to be honest) and also round.

I know that it is round because I saw these charts in a magazine at the dentist showing all different shapes of faces, including heart-shaped, egg-shaped, diamond-shaped, turnip-shaped, square-shaped and round.

Mine is definitely round. Unfortunately. Round-faced people tend to have blobby noses, which is what I have got.

The school I go to is Ruskin Manor. It is not the school I would have chosen if I had had any choice. If I had had any choice I would have chosen a boarding school because I think a boarding school would be fun and also it would take me away from Slimey. Anything that took me away from Slimey would have to be a good thing. I did ask Mum if I could go to one but she just said, "Over my dead body". She was really pleased when I got to Ruskin because it's the one she wanted for me. She says all the others are rough.

Ruskin is OK, I suppose, though we have simply stacks of homework, which Mum needless to say approves of. On the other hand, I have only been there for three weeks so there is no telling how I might feel by the end of term. Anything could happen. Our class teacher, Mr Sherwood, who at the moment seems quite nice, could for instance suddenly grow fangs, or the

Mr Sherwood   Head

Head Teacher turn out to be a werewolf.

I mean, you just never know. (The Head Teacher is called Mrs Hoad. What kind of name is Hoad? It sounds rather sinister to me.)

Skinny Melon

My best friend Melanie also goes to Ruskin. Her surname is Skinner and she is very tall and thin so I call her Skinny Melon, or Skinbag, or sometimes just Skin. John Lloyd, who is a boy in our class, said last week that we were the Long and the Short of it, but that is only because Skinny Melon is so tall, not because I am short.

9

This is me standing by her

Skin's face shape wasn't shown in the magazine. It's long and thin, the same as the rest of her. Sausage-shaped, I suppose you would call it. Like a Frankfurter.

Me and Skin have been best friends since Year 5 and we are going to go on being best friends "through thick and thin and come what may". We have made a pledge and signed it and buried it in a polythene food bag under an apple tree in my back garden. If ever we decide to stop being best friends we will have to dig up the pledge and solemnly burn it. This is what we have agreed on.

Where I live is 141 Arethusa Road, London W5. W5 is Ealing and it is right at the end of the red and green lines on the Underground.

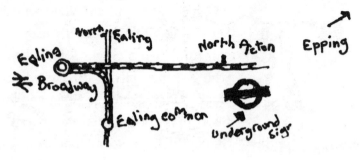

Skin and I once decided to go and see what Epping was like as we had heard there was some forest there, but we got on the wrong train and went to a place called Fairlop instead.

Ealing doesn't have any forests, just a bit of scrubby common which you can walk to from Arethusa Road. There is also a park where Skinny Melon and me take her dog Lulu to meet other dogs. I wish more than anything I could have a dog! Well almost more than anything.

What I would wish more than anything is alas impossible as it would mean turning the clock back, which is something you cannot do unless you happen to be living in a science fiction novel where people travel into the past and change things. I would like to travel into the past and change things. That is what I would like more than anything else. But after that the next thing that I would like is a dog.

Any sort of dog would do. Big dog, small dog, I wouldn't mind.

11

Why I am suddenly starting to write this diary is that Mrs James, who is our English teacher, said that it would be a good thing to do. She said there are several reasons for keeping a diary. These are some that I can remember:

a) It is good practice for when it comes to writing essays etc. for school.

b) It is a record of one's life and will be interesting to look back on when one is old.

c) It is a social document (for historical purposes, etc.).

d) It can help to clear out the cupboard.

When Mrs James said about clearing out the cupboard, we did not immediately understand what she meant and some people started giggling and pretending to open cupboard doors and take out cans of fruit and stuff and chuck it away, but Mrs James said the cupboard she was talking about was "the cupboard in your head". She said that sometimes the cupboard in your head gets all clogged up with bits and pieces that worry you or upset you or make you angry, and that writing them down in a diary helps to get rid of them. She said, "We've all got a lot of clutter that needs clearing out." She told us to go home and think about it – to look into our cupboards and see what was there.

Amanda Miles told me next day that she'd looked into her cupboard and as far as she could see it was pretty well empty, except for the grudge she still had against Mr Good at Juniors who made her go and stand in the front hall for throwing paint water at Andy Innes when it wasn't her. She said she didn't think that was enough to start writing a diary about.

"I mean, are you going to?" she said.

To which I just made mumbling noises, since there are some things you can't talk about to other people, and certainly not to Amanda Miles. The thing in my cupboard is one of them.

Slimey Roland is the thing in my cupboard.

I'd do anything to get rid of him. I wish he'd go and walk under a bus. I expect Mum would be sad for a bit, but she'd get over it. She can't really love him. Nobody could. He's a total and utter dweeb.

I nearly had a heart attack when Mum said she was going to marry him. I mean, I really just couldn't believe it. I thought she'd got better taste. I told her so and she slapped me and then burst into tears and said she was sorry but why did I have to be so selfish and unpleasant all the time?

I'm not selfish and unpleasant. I don't think I am. But it's enough to make you, when your mum goes and marries a total dweeb. And I had to go to their rotten grotty old wedding, which wasn't even a proper wedding, not the actual marrying part. Just Mum and Slime, and me and the Skinbag, who came to keep me company, and Aunt Jilly, who is Mum's sister, and this man who was doing it. Marrying them, I mean.

When he'd finished he said that now they could kiss

each other and they did and I looked at Skin and pulled this being-sick face (at which I am rather good) and Skin told me afterwards that I was horrid to do such a thing at my mum's wedding. It's all right for her. I know she hasn't got a dad, but who'd want Slimey?

One of the worst things about him is his name… Roland Butter. Can you imagine? I thought at first it was just one of his stupid jokes (he's always making stupid jokes, like: Where do pigs leave their cars? At porking meters. Ha ha ha, I *don't* think). Mum, however, said no, he really was called Roland Butter. He's an artist, sort of. He draws these yucky pictures of elves and teddy bears and stuff for little kids' books and he has this headed paper with a drawing of a roll and butter on it. Mum thinks it's brilliant but that's because she's besotted. If you ask me, it's utterly pathetic and I am certainly not going to change my name to Butter, which is what Mum would like me to do. Cherry Butter! I ask you! How could you get anywhere with a name like that?

Mum's name is Pat, and guess what? He calls her Butterpat. It's just so embarrassing.

Dad used to call her Patty. She was Patty and he was Gregg, unless they were having one of their rows and then they didn't call each other anything at all except names which I am not going to write in this diary in case it is ever published. It is true that Mum and Dad did have rows quite often, but what I can't understand is why they couldn't just kiss and make up like Skinny and I do?

We had this really awful row once, me and Skin, about a book I'd lent her which she'd gone and lost by leaving it on a bus and then refused to buy a new one because she said I'd never paid her back the money she'd lent me ages ago when we'd gone swimming and I'd left my purse behind, which definitely and positively was not true. We had this absolutely mega row and swore never to speak to each other again, but life wasn't the same without Skinny, and Skinny said it wasn't the same without me, and so after a bit, like about a week, we made it up and we've been best friends ever since. Why couldn't Mum and Dad do that?

Dad's living in Southampton now. It's near the New Forest and is really nice, but it takes forever to get there. I can't go out with him every weekend like I used to when he and Mum first split up and he was still living in London. Then, he'd come and pick me up and we'd do all sorts of things together – McDonald's, museums, the waxworks. It was really fun. After he got this job and moved to Southampton it meant I could only properly see him in school holidays.

I could have gone with him if I'd wanted. If I'd really wanted. I bet I could. I only stayed with Mum because I thought she'd be lonely. But then she went and met Slimey Roland at some stupid party and they went and got married and now she's totally loopy about him and I'm the one that's lonely, not Mum. So I could have gone with Dad.

Except that Dad's got a new wife called Rosemary, and he's totally loopy about *her*, so maybe he wouldn't want me either. Maybe nobody wants me. Mum says she does but how could she go and marry this creep if that was the case? He's really slimy. Look at him!

Ha! He's not the only one that can draw. There's nothing to it. That is exactly how he looks. Straggly hair and a beard and this long, droopy face like a damp dishcloth. And he's all freckled and gingery with white skin like a mushroom. Ugh! Whatever does Mum see in him?

She says that if I love her I'll try and love Slimey, for her sake. I've *tried*. But how can you love someone who has freckles and makes these awful jokes all the time? Another thing he does, he shoves these cards under the bedroom door while I'm asleep. It's really creepy. I find them lying there waiting for me when I wake up. They're all covered in these soppy drawings which I think are supposed to be messages. I don't bother to read them. I just chuck them straight into the waste-paper basket.

I know why he's doing it. He's so transparent it's pathetic. He's trying to impress me. Well, some hopes! I just think he's a total nerd.

Mum's best friend Carol that she was at school with and who is my godmother, but who has now gone to live in Austin, Texas, alas (though she has promised to send me a real American baseball bat for my Christmas present), told me that Mum and Dad had become very unhappy together on account of "developing in different directions", which meant they didn't really have anything in common any more – apart from me, that is, but it seems children don't count.

Carol said that it's lovely for Mum to be with Slimey because they are both in the same business, with Slimey being an illustrator of children's books and Mum being something called a copy editor, which means going through books that other people have written and making sure they've got their facts right and have put all the commas and fullstops in the right places and haven't called their heroine Anne Smith on one page and Anne Jones on another.

All I can say is that it may be lovely for Mum, but it isn't very lovely for me. And if writing a diary means clearing Slimey Roland out of the cupboard then I am ALL FOR IT.

Tuesday

He made another of his awful jokes this morning. He said, "What's a cannibal's favourite game?" To humour him and keep Mum happy I said, "What is a cannibal's favourite game?" though in fact I already knew the answer because it was a joke that was going round when I was in Year 5, for goodness' sake. So he beams into his beard, all jolly ho ho, and says, "Swallow my leader!" and Mum groans and rolls her eyes, but in a way that means she thinks it's really quite funny, and I just give this tight little smile and get on with my breakfast. It is extremely irritating when grown-ups behave in this infantile fashion. Doesn't he realise he's making a complete idiot of himself?

I have decided to record occasionally what I eat for dinner, because this school's canteen must I think be the secret weapon of someone who has a hate thing against children. Skinny asked Mr Sherwood the other day why he didn't eat there. She said, "Is it because you don't want to be poisoned?" Mr Sherwood said that at his age being poisoned was a distinct possibility. He said, "My digestive system is no longer geared to the hazards of a school canteen."

If that isn't an admission, what is???

I told Mum what Mr Sherwood said. I actually put it to her: "If you don't want to lose me, then maybe I ought to take sandwiches?" All she said was, "Oh, Cherry, don't be silly! What do you want sandwiches for? You're spoilt for choice, you people! In my day it was wet mash and soggy greens and that was that, like it or lump it. Now it's more like a five-star hotel."

I can only conclude that Mum has never been to a five-star hotel. I asked her to name one and she said,

"Oh, the Ritz! The Savoy!" I bet the Ritz and the Savoy don't dish up plates of disgusting white worms in congealed blood and call it spaghetti. That's what I had today, white worms in blood. Utterly foul.

Wednesday

Brown worms today. Brown worms in something-I-won't-put-a-name-to as it makes me feel sick. And anyway, I don't know how to spell it. Yeeeeeurgh!!!!!

Thursday

There are times when I hate Mum for the way she treats me. Skinny Melon couldn't walk home with me after school today because, guess what? Her mum was taking her to buy a bra! Skinny Melon who is as thin as a piece of thread! Not a bump to be seen. Not even the beginnings of a bump. I am practically a double-D cup compared to her. I mean, she doesn't even get on the chart! But her mum is so nice. It's like she went out and bought her brother a razor for his birthday even though he hadn't got anything to shave, hardly. So the Melon hasn't got anything to put in a bra, but still her mum takes her seriously.

She even takes the Blob seriously, for heaven's sake!

The Blob is Skin's sister and rather immature, as one tends to be at only eight years old. She is still at the stage of asking these dippy questions such as "Where do babies come from?" Skinny's mum never fobs her off with yucky stories about storks or gooseberry bushes but treats her like a real person and tells her the truth. That's how grown-ups ought to behave. It is very patronising and hurtful when they laugh at you behind your back, which is what Mum and Slimey do. I'm not saying they do it all the time but it is what they did tonight.

When I got back from school, Slimey was up in his studio (the back bedroom, which ought by rights to have been mine) and I took the opportunity to suggest to Mum in *strictest confidence* that maybe it was time I, too, started to wear a bra. I said, "If the Melon does and I don't, I shall get the most terrific inferiority complex… It could stunt the whole of my future sex-life." Mum said, "Oh, my goodness, we can't have that! But really why you all want to grow up so quickly I can't imagine."

I said, "Why? Isn't it any fun being grown-up?" and she said, "Sometimes it is, sometimes it isn't." So, as I said to her, where's the difference? She needn't think it's all fun being a child, because I can assure her it most definitely is not. Not when the parents go and split up and the child is just left like an old bit of baggage. "Who is going to take it? You or me?" And then they both go and get married again and probably wish there wasn't any child because really it is such a nuisance, always being so selfish and unpleasant. "Why did we ever have it in the first place?"

If Mum thinks that's fun, she must have a very strange sense of humour, that's all I can say.

Anyway, she agreed we could go in on Saturday maybe and buy me a bra, so that was all right. In fact I felt quite warm towards her and thought that in spite of divorcing Dad and marrying the Slime she was every bit as nice a Mum as Skinny's. I thought of what Carol had said about her and Dad growing apart and I thought that perhaps it was just one of those things that happened and that it wasn't really her fault. I even half made up my mind that in future I would try to be nicer to her and forgive her for what she'd done.

And THEN she had to go and blow it all. She went and betrayed me with *him*.

What happened, I'd gone upstairs to wash and she was in the back bedroom with Slimey and she'd left the door a bit open. I wasn't eavesdropping, but even if I had been, so what? I think one has a right to know what people are saying about one behind one's back. What I heard Mum say was, "Hasn't got anything there!" and then go off into these idiotic peals of laughter. I hate her for that. I shall never trust her again. I bet old Slimey thought it was *really* funny.

And anyway, I've got more than Skinny has!

Friday

There is a girl at school called Avril Roper whose dog has just had puppies. She said if anyone wants one they can have one free because the puppies were a mistake and her mum is only interested in them going to people who will love them, not in making money. I tore home like the wind and burst into the kitchen and yelled, "Mum, Mum, can we have a puppy? They're going free! And they're small ones, Mum!" I said this because last time I found some puppies, which was before she married Slimey, they were in a pet shop and cost £50 each and were some sort of mixture that was going to grow as tall as the kitchen table and eat us out of house and home. So naturally I thought as these were free, and were tiny, she'd say yes right away, no problem.

Instead she just laughed, sort of nervously, and said, "Puppies are always small, to my knowledge."

I said, "Yes, but these are going to stay small. Their mum is a Jack Russell and their dad was a Yorkshire terrier."

You can't get much smaller than a Yorkshire terrier. And anyway, she promised. As good as. After Dad left and Mum and me were on our own she said, "We'll get a dog to keep us company." But she never did. Now here was I offering her one free, so why didn't she jump at it?

Because of Slimey Roland, that's why. I said, "You promised!" and this shifty look came into her eyes and she didn't want to meet my gaze, which is a sure sign of guilt. She said, "I don't think I actually promised." I said, "You did! You promised!" Mum said, "I may have mentioned it as a possibility. That's all." I said, "Well, now it is a possibility! They're going for free!"

And then Mum sighed and said, "Cherry, I'd love a dog as much as you would, but how can we? You know Roly's allergic." I said, "Allergic to dogs?" How can anyone be allergic to dogs? I said, "I know he has hay fever." But hay fever is pollen. Mum said, "I'm afraid it's not just hay fever. The poor man's allergic to all kinds of things – dust, pollution, house mites…"

And dogs. He just would be, wouldn't he? He's that sort of person. All wimpy and sniffly and red-eyed. So Mum has to break her promise just because of him!

Saturday

That creep shoved another note under my door. Something about a tortoise. I don't want a rotten tortoise! I want a dog. Mum promised me.

This morning we went into the shops and I got a couple of bras, one white and one pink. I suppose they're all right, but it's all gone a bit sour now that I know she and Slime have been sniggering about it. I keep picturing them lying in bed together having this good laugh.

I chucked his note into the waste-paper basket along with all the others. If he doesn't stop doing it, it'll soon be full to overflowing. Mum said today that we are going to have a new regime. She said, "I looked into your bedroom yesterday and it's like a pigsty," to which I instantly retorted that as a matter of fact pigs left to themselves are extremely clean and intelligent animals. It's only horrible farmers that make them dirty by not allowing them to lead natural lives. To which Mum said, thinking herself very clever, "Well in future I am going to leave you to yourself and we shall see how clean and intelligent you are. From here on in –" (that is a phrase she has picked up from Carol my godmother, who has picked it up in Austin, Texas) "– from here on in I wash my hands of your bedroom. You can take sole responsibility for it. Right?"

I just humped a shoulder, feeling generally disgruntled on account of Mum breaking her promise about the dog. Mum said again, "Right?" and I muttered "Right," and Slimey Roland did his best to catch my eye across the table and wink, but I refused to take any notice.

Later on, Avril Roper rang to find out if we were going to have one of the puppies. I didn't want to say no, so I said we hadn't yet decided, and she said me and Skinny could go round and see them sometime if I liked. She said, "They're so *sweet*. You won't be able to resist them. You can hold them in the palm of your hand!"

So then I rushed back to Mum and said, "Mum, they're so tiny you can hold them in the palm of your hand! Oh, Mum, can't we have one? Please?" thinking that if I really begged hard enough she wouldn't be able to say no, but she was obviously feeling in a mean mood because all she did was snap at me. She said, "I already told you, the answer is no! Roly's health happens to be of more importance to me than a dog. I'm sorry, but there it is."

I gave her this really venomous look as I slunk out of the room.

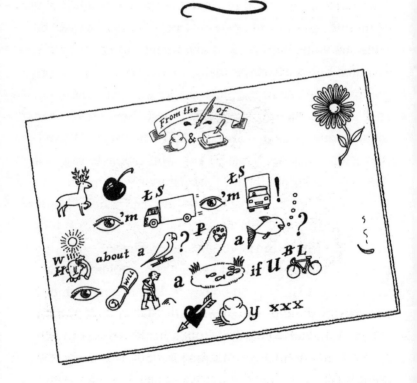

Sunday

It is after breakfast and I am writing this sitting on my bed. If Mum doesn't do my bedroom soon the waste-paper basket will be overflowing with notes from Slimey Roland. I am on strike. Mum *always* used to do my bedroom.

I used to help Dad clean the car but Slimey hasn't got one because he can't drive. And Mum can't have one because Slimey won't let her. He says they pollute the environment and we all have to walk or use bicycles. I am not going to help him clean his bicycle!!! He looks like a total idiot riding about with his helmet on and his soppy little cycling shorts. Like a stick insect with his head stuck in a goldfish bowl.

Anyway, I help with laying the table and putting things away and doing the wiping up. She won't let me do the washing up any more because she says I use too much washing-up liquid (Greencare, natch. Slimey won't have ordinary Fairy liquid in the house, you bet he won't. He's a complete nutter. He goes round reading all the labels and checking the lists of ingredients and spying on me and Mum to make sure we don't buy anything that might punch holes in the ozone layer).

Another reason Mum won't let me do the washing up is that she says I cause too many breakages. So now Slimey gets to do it and he does it ever so s-l-o-w-l-y and c-a-r-e-f-u-l-l-y and nearly drives me mad.

Dad never used to help in the kitchen, it was one of the things that he and Mum had rows about. But Dad used to go out to work all day. Slimey works at home (if it can be called work, just drawing pictures of elves). It's only fair that he should help.

It wouldn't have been fair if Dad had had to. I don't think it would. When I was little and Dad was in an office we were really really happy. He and Mum hardly ever had rows or shouted at each other. It was only when Dad got made redundant and couldn't find another job and had to go and do the mini-cabbing that it all became horrible. That was when the rows started, because of Dad having to go out and do something he didn't like while Mum just went on sitting at home and reading her books. Of course she was being paid money to do it but it wasn't the same as having to go mini-cabbing. That was what Dad said.

One thing about Slimey, he is interested in Mum's work. Sometimes he reads the books and they discuss them together. Also, he and Mum don't have rows. Yet. But they sit and hold hands and do a lot of kissing and I can't stand it! I hate to think of them holding hands and kissing all day while I'm at school. It makes me feel sick. Kissing with a *beard*. I hate beards.

It's eleven o'clock now and I'm going to go down the road and fetch their Sunday papers for them, which is another of the jobs I have to do that Mum doesn't take into consideration when she goes on about my bedroom. When I come back I might ring Skinny Melon and see if she's going to take Lulu up the park. Or I might ring Avril and find out how the puppies are. Imagine having a dog all of your own! I could have, if it weren't for Slimey. He's in the back bedroom at the moment, drawing elves, and Mum is downstairs on the word processor, writing to her friend, Carol in Austin, Texas. They write to each other every single week! It's almost unbelievable. What on earth do they find to say???

Sunday 27 September

My dear Carol,

Lovely to have all your news and so glad things are working out for you. Just forget all about Martin. He was a jerk and you are well rid of him. Some people are better apart. Take Gregg and me, for instance. We made each other utterly wretched, yet I couldn't be happier with Roly! I'm sure you'll soon meet someone else, though I confess I live in dread that it will turn out to be some big handsome Texan and that you'll settle down for good and all in the States! It's a long way to come and visit…

You ask how Cherry is getting on at her new school. Quite well, as far as I can make out, though she doesn't say very much. The thing she is most vociferous about is the food! She is becoming terribly faddy, but I suppose it's her age. I seem to recall when I was eleven going through a phase when I wanted to eat nothing but Mars Bars. Ah, those were the days! One Mars Bar, one KitKat, one Penguin biscuit, all gobbled up before the morning break and not a spare inch of flesh to be seen! Of course I wouldn't let Cherry eat stuff like that. Roly, fortunately, is educating me in the way to healthy living. No more junk food! No more snacks! In fact I think we shall all end up as veggies.

I wish I could say that Cherry's attitude towards Roland had changed for the better, but she is still very cold. It's so unfair, because he tries so hard. He keeps sending her these really charming little cards with coded messages in the form of pictures. Any other child would be delighted. But I see Cherry simply throws them in her waste-paper basket. It's so ungracious. As a result I am refusing to clean up her bedroom for her. She can jolly well do it herself!

She is a bit peeved at the moment because a girl at school has offered her a puppy and she has taken it into her head that I actually promised her she could have one. I'm sure I only said that I would think about it. Anyway, as it happens it's just not possible as poor Roly is seriously allergic. He's going to start digging a pond in the back garden so that we can have some fish. I think she'll like that.

Oh, I must tell you! It was so funny the other day. Cherry, as you may remember, has this friend called Melanie who is like a beanpole, and Melanie, my dear, was going out to buy a bra! So naturally Cherry decided that she wanted one, too, and we had to trundle out yesterday morning to get her a couple. But the joke is, she has nothing there! As flat as the proverbial pancake! Well, it probably makes her feel sophisticated and Roly says we mustn't laugh as one is very sensitive to these things when one is young.

Roly really is a most extraordinarily understanding sort of person. And sympathetic! Far more than I am when she starts playing up. She has really been trying my patience just recently. But Roly never loses his temper. He never allows himself to be goaded. That is why it makes me so angry, the way Cherry treats him. He could be such a wonderful dad to her! If only she would let him. I am hoping that the goldfish will do the trick…

Write soon! All love,

Patsy

Monday

Dad rang last night. He said his new job is keeping him really busy. He is having to work at weekends and that is why he can't come up to London to see me. But maybe I can go and stay with him at half-term. He is going to speak to Mum. She'd better say yes! It's the least she can do, now she's gone and broken her promise about letting me have a dog.

Old Slimey is digging up the back garden. He's trying to get me interested in goldfish and suchlike junk. Huh! He needn't think that will make up for not having one of Avril's puppies. How can you communicate with a fish?

Tuesday

Slime stew for dinner today. It had a cardboard lid which I thought they had forgotten to remove before heating but John Lloyd said it was pastry. All I can say is it didn't taste like it.

I told Skin about Slimey and his stupid goldfish and she said that as a matter of fact you can communicate with goldfish "in a sort of way". She said that they get used to you and will come to the surface for food. I said, "Oh, brilliant! Do they speak to you? Do they play games? Can you take them for walks?" Skinny told me not to be stupid. She said, "A fish is not a dog." I said, "I know that, thank you very much." She then informed me that I was just being horrible "because the fish were Roly's idea and nothing that he thinks of is ever right for you."

Cheek! What does she know about it?

On the way home from school we had a bit of an argument. Well, a bit of a quarrel really, I suppose. The Skinbag revealed to me that she thinks wearing a bra makes it look as if she has a real bust. Ho ho! What a laugh! I told her she was kidding herself and she got quite snappish and said, "Well, you needn't imagine you'd win any prizes! Two goose pimples is all you've got."

I thought that was uncalled for. I mean, that was a very personal sort of remark to make. You don't expect it from someone calling herself your best friend. We grouched at each other all the way home. Skinny said I was a midget, which isn't true because there are at least two people in our class that are shorter than me, and I said she didn't have any waist, which is true, and she can't deny it. She hasn't any shape at all. Then she said I had a nose like a squashed tomato, and I said she had a face like a Frankfurter, and by the time we got to her road we weren't talking any more, just stomping along in a simmering silence.

I went on simmering all through tea, because I think it's good to let people stew in their own juice for a bit otherwise they think you're crawling. I mean, I didn't see why I should be the one to ring when she was just as much to blame as I was. In fact she was the one who started it, going on about the goldfish. If she hadn't gone on about goldfish, I wouldn't have said that about her kidding herself over her bust. I know the goldfish were earlier, but it really maddened me her saying what she said. That is, about me being horrible to Slime. She ought to try living with him.

For instance, all the time I'm simmering he's sitting there at the table cracking his fingers, which is this thing that he does. Crack, crack, crack, going off like pistol shots. And then he starts making more of his stupid jokes like, "What do you get if you cross a witch with an ice cube? A cold spell," until I couldn't stand it any more so I went and tried ringing the Skinbag, only her number was engaged, but then seconds later she rang me and said she'd tried to get me before but *my* number was engaged, and I said, "That was me trying to get you," and she said, "Oh, right," and there was this awkward pause, and then we both spoke together in a rush.

I said, "I'm really sorry I said that about your face looking like a Frankfurter," and Skinny said, "I apologise for saying you were a midget." And so then we were friends again and started talking about our maths homework.

Why couldn't Mum and Dad be like that?

Wednesday

Scum and matter pie, and a dollop of cold sick. Well, that's what it looked like. Skinny and me have this theory about school dinners. We reckon they take all the stuff that's scraped off the plates and recycle it. Then they dish it back up as slime or slush or squidgy messes and give it fancy names such as Cheese and Onion Tart or Lentil Bake. No wonder the staff don't eat with us. Mrs James says it's to avoid the rabble (meaning us). She says, "We like a bit of peace and quiet."

I bet! They like a bit of proper food and not regurgitated yuck.

Thursday

Rat hot-pot. Slimey Roland wouldn't have touched it! He's a cranky vegetarian. He said to me yesterday, "You

wouldn't eat a puppy, would you? So why eat a lamb?"
He has a nerve, talking about puppies. If it weren't for
him I could have one. I'm going to see them tomorrow.

Friday

I saw them. They are gorgeous! They look like little
balls of fluff.

← Avril's puppies

But all of them have been spoken for except one. I
came rushing home to tell Mum and she said, "Oh,
Cherry, don't start that again!" in a pleading sort of
voice, which shows she's got a guilty conscience. I said,
"But Mum, they're so gorgeous!" and at that point
Slimey Roland came barging into the conversation. He
said, "Oh, Cherry Pie, I'm so sorry! It's all my fault.
Don't go on at your mum!"

I hope he isn't going to make a habit of calling me
Cherry Pie. It makes me want to throw up.

Saturday

Slime said to me at breakfast this morning, "By the way, little lambs are rather gorgeous, too."

What's that to do with anything? I'm not asking for a lamb!

Sunday 2 October

Dearest Carol,

Just a quickie as I have to go and help Roly with the pond. It's coming along apace! Cherry still refuses to have anything to do with it but she'll come round. When we actually get the fish she won't be able to resist it. She's still resentful of the fact that she can't have a dog, and I must say that I would rather like one myself, and so would Roly. He is not opposed to dogs, in fact he loves them, as he loves all small creatures (including cross-grained eleven year olds!) but we simply can't run the risk of setting off his allergy. I think left to himself he might weaken, but I'm not having him ruin his health just to keep Cherry happy. I know it was upsetting for her when Gregg and I separated; on the other hand she is extremely lucky to have a step-dad as warm and funny and caring as Roly.

He'll win her over in the end. I know he will!

Lots of love,

Patsy

PS I'm ashamed to say that I still haven't got around to telling Cherry about you-know-what. I'm terrified of breaking it to her in case she reacts badly. So far I've managed to keep it hidden by wearing baggy T-shirts but it's reached the point where not even the baggiest of T-shirts will hide the bulge! Fortunately, at the moment, she is so wrapped up in her own affairs that she probably wouldn't notice anyway. But I can't afford to leave it very much longer. As Roly says, it's not fair on her.

Monday

Janetta Barnes found a slug in her salad today. She's taken it home to show her mum. I'm hoping her mum will sue someone and then maybe we'll get to have better dinners.

Tuesday

We all had to line up in the hall at break while Mrs James and Miss Burgess walked up and down looking at us. They said they were looking for interesting faces for the Christmas play. I have been picked to be an angel! A *singing* angel.

I rushed home to tell Mum, thinking she'd be pleased, and all she did was laugh and say, "You? An angel?" I said, "Miss Burgess says I have an angelic face." Mum said, "Yes, you do! I'll grant you that. Isn't it strange how looks can be so deceiving?" I told her that it was a play and that I was going to be acting. I said, "And singing as well, as a matter of fact." Mum said, "*Singing?*" That really impressed her, I could tell. Mum never knew that I could sing. But I can!

Wednesday

All the puppies have gone! Oh, and they were so beeeeeeauuuutiful! I hope they've been taken by people who will be kind to them and look after them. If I had a dog and it had puppies I would never give any of them away, ever, because you can't trust what people might be going to do with them. There are some people that are just so cruel it is unbelievable. Avril says her mum checked most carefully and they have all gone to good homes where they will be loved, but nobody could love them as much as I would have done!

Curried compost-heap for dinner today. I found what looked like the remains of a beetle in mine. Janetta says she showed the slug that she found to her mum and her mum said it wasn't a slug but a bit of oberjene (?) but Janetta is still sure it was a slug. She thinks what happened was it got squashed in her bag on the way home, on account of all the homework we have to lug about with us, and had therefore gone a bit flat. I think her mum just didn't want to admit that it was a slug. I've noticed that whenever you tell parents anything bad about school, like rotten school dinners or one of the teachers having a go at you for doing something when it wasn't you, they always take the teacher's side and say, "Well, you must have done *something*", or "You must be exaggerating". They hate to admit you could ever be right and a teacher might be wrong. I'm dead sure it was a beetle I found but it's no use taking it home as Mum would only say it was a mustard seed or something.

I forgot to record that Skinny was not picked to be anything in the Christmas play, I suppose because a long, thin face is perhaps not as interesting as a round, blobby one, but fortunately she doesn't mind as she has no wish to be an actress. She says even if they had picked her she wouldn't have wanted to be in it. It is a relief that she is not jealous, but I have to say that on the whole Skinny has a very nice nature. She has promised to come to one of the performances and cheer me on.

Thursday

Today I ate a plate of cold sick with dubious-looking objects floating in it. I had this vision of one of the cooks throwing up in the kitchen and someone running at her with a basin yelling, "Don't waste anything, don't waste anything! Recycle!" Skinny Melon says I am disgusting but I just happen to have this very vivid sort of imagination.

Skinny came back with me for tea after school and it was so embarrassing, I didn't know where to put myself. Slimey Roland was there, all covered in mud from digging this stupid pond he keeps on about. He looked such a sight! I could have died when he came and sat down with us at the table. I was so ashamed of him. And then he started making these awful jokes, the way he does, like, "What do you call two spiders who've just got married? Newly Webs!" and "What's full of sandwiches and hides in a bell tower? The Lunch Pack of Notre Dame!" I mean, they're just not funny. I don't think they are.

Skinny was really brilliant and kept groaning and giggling and making like she was amused. She was only doing it out of pity for me, I could tell. It was nice of her, but then he started to think he was some kind of big comedy star and just went on and on till I wanted to scream. Skinny actually choked at one point and I thought she was going to suffocate, she went so red. I expect the reason she choked was he was being so *ex-cru-cia-ting*.

I apologised to her afterwards. I said, "He's really grungy, isn't he?" I thought we could have a nice hate-Slimey session but Skinny wouldn't play. She has this thing about fathers, which is because hers went and died when she was really young so that she never properly knew him and as a result she thinks even a dad like Slime is better than no dad at all. I told her that a) he wasn't my dad. I already had a dad, thank you very much. Just because he isn't living with us doesn't make him not my dad any more and b) she'd change her mind quickly enough if Slimey Roland married *her* mum and went to live in *her* house.

I said, "Imagine listening to those yucky jokes every day!" Skinny said that she would be quite happy listening to yucky jokes. She agreed that they were yucky but said she thought that Slime was "an ace joke-teller". I said "Oh, do you?" and she said, yes, she did, so I said, "Well, I don't. I think he's pathetic." I said, "He's a wimp and a weed and he sniffles." To which Skinny retorted, "So what?" She then had the nerve to tell me that I wasn't being fair.

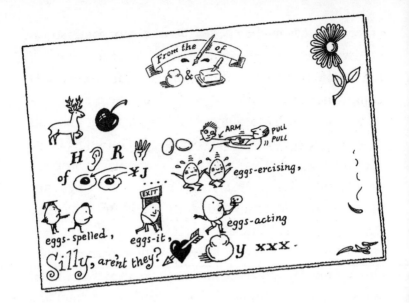

From the ✒ of 🥚 & 🧈

eggs-ercising,

eggs-spelled,   eggs-it,   eggs-acting

Silly, aren't they?   ...y xxx.

Friday

The Skinbag must be mad. She said to me today that she thinks Slimey Roland is "really nice". She also said, "Is your mum going to have a baby?" which made me want to knock her head off. I said, "No, of course she isn't! What makes you think that?" and she said, " 'Cos she looks as if she is." So I said, "Oh?" raising both my eyebrows up into my fringe to show I was displeased. "What exactly is that supposed to mean?" She said, "Well she's all kind of bulgy round the middle."

I told her I'd poke her eyes out if she said anything like that about my mum again, so then she said, "Sorry, I'm sure," meaning she wasn't sorry at all, and went into a huff and shut up. We haven't talked all the rest of the day.

How dare she say Mum's bulgy round the middle? That would be like me saying her mum had sticking-out teeth, which she has.

← Skinny's Mum's gnashers

But I wouldn't ever say it because it would be rude. And anyway, what would Mum want a baby for? When she's already got me?

Saturday

I've been thinking about what Skinny said. I have a horrible feeling that it might be true. Mum *is* looking bulgy. I suddenly saw it when she was getting off the bus. And this morning after we'd done all the shopping and were going to go and have what Slimey calls "coffee and cakies". (He spends so much time drawing pictures of elves that his mind has gone completely infantile.) I couldn't help noticing that they spent ages standing outside a baby shop gorming at all the prams and potties and carry-cots. They didn't realise I was watching them. They thought I was too busy giving money to a person that was collecting for anti-vivisection, and I *was* giving them money, because I think that anyone that experiments on animals ought to be experimented on themselves, but at the same time I was watching Mum and Slimey. They had their arms round each other's waists! Pathetic, really. Mum is going to be thirty-six next year, and I know for a fact that Slime is even older. I don't think people of that age ought to go about in public with their arms round each other, I think it looks really naff. Especially when one of them is your own mother.

I don't think I could bear it if Mum was going to have another baby. But surely she would have told me? Maybe she is just suffering from middle-age spread.

While we were doing the shopping I looked at some aubergines (which is how it is spelt, not oberjenes as I originally thought) and they are not in the least like slugs, more like big purple eggs, so I really don't know what Janetta's mum was talking about.

After lunch Aunt Jilly and Uncle Ivo came and brought their new baby with them. It is a horrible thing, all sicky and stinky and does nothing but bawl.

Mum and Slimey both drooled over it. Slime kept giving it his bony old finger to hold and making these silly baby noises. I personally think you ought to talk to babies sensibly, in proper language, so that they can learn things. I don't see any point in filling their heads with all this gooey yuck. I mean, if they grow up thinking that stuff like "Doo doo doo" is how people communicate, for goodness' sake, it's just going to retard them. It stands to reason. They left me alone with it for a few

↑Baby

minutes and I went up to it and said, "Good afternoon. How are you today?" and it actually looked at me quite intelligently. I don't expect it knew what I was saying, but I bet the words have gone into its head and I bet they'll be some of the first words it ever speaks. I bet they'll get a surprise one day when it sits up in its pram and says good afternoon to them.

"Good afternoon. How are you today?"

They won't know it's me they have to thank.

I'm getting more and more worried about Mum. She and Aunt Jilly went into the kitchen together to look at a plant that keeps shrivelling and they were there for simply ages so I went after them to find out what they were doing and as soon as she saw me, Mum gave Aunt Jilly this warning glance and they both stopped talking, but not before I'd heard what they were saying. Well, what Mum was saying. She was saying, "Yes, I know, I'm really going to have to pluck up the courage and tell her."

It doesn't sound good.

9 October

Dear Carol,

Many thanks for your lovely long letter! I'm afraid
this is going to be another shortish one as we've been
out walking all day on Hampstead Heath and I am
whacked. Getting too old and fat!!!

The answer to your question, which I know you're
going to ask, is no... I haven't yet broken the news to
Cherry. Yes, yes, I accept that I'm a total coward, but I
am going to do it tomorrow afternoon when she gets
in from school. Roly has to go away for the night – he
is doing a talk to some mixed infants way up in the
north of England – and so it will be a good
opportunity. Just Cherry and me on our own. I think
she might take it better that way.

We all really enjoyed ourselves today. It was a
lovely family outing, the sort of thing we ought to do
more often. We took our food with us and had a good
old-fashioned picnic! It was Roly's idea, and he
prepared all the goodies. He was really imaginative –
and it was all vegetarian! Vegetable samosas, sausage
rolls made with vegebangers, vegetable kebabs, soya

desserts. I am quite being won over, and I think Cherry is, too. At any rate, she gobbled everything up. I don't believe she even realised that the sausage rolls weren't made with real sausages!

Altogether it was an absolutely super day. It gives me hope that Cherry is coming round at last. I am just keeping my fingers crossed that hearing about you-know-what doesn't set her back.

Jilly and Ivo came over yesterday with little Sammy, and at first Cherry was very cool, very aloof, refused even to look at him. But then we left them alone together for a few minutes, just to see what would happen, and she couldn't resist! Roly reports that she was nattering away nineteen to the dozen. So I think when she gets used to the idea she'll be fine.

She has been asked to take the part of an angel in the school nativity play, if you can believe it. An angel! Cherry! She is also going to sing. I don't know if you have ever heard your god-daughter sing? It is not an experience I would recommend! She has a voice rather like a hyena. I only hope they don't discover their error and give the part to someone else because she is terribly puffed up and looking forward to it. I wouldn't like her little bubble to be burst.

Her friend Melanie came to tea the other day. She is a nice child; steady and reliable. Cherry occasionally tries bossing her but fortunately Melanie can hold her own. I think that's why the friendship has lasted.

Melanie won't stand for any nonsense! Roly was there and kept everyone in stitches, clowning around and generally playing the fool. He is absolutely, instinctively marvellous with kids. I think Cherry was quite proud of him. She certainly ought to have been.

There! This letter hasn't turned out so short after all. Next time I will report how she takes the news about Mum's big secret...

All my love,

Patsy

Sunday

Today we all trailed half-way across London to go for a picnic on Hampstead Heath. On account of Slimey Roland refusing to pollute the environment, we had to go by tube. That meant taking the Central line to Tottenham Court Road, which is 13 stops, and then hanging about for ever waiting for a northern line to Hampstead, which was another seven. What a pathetic way to travel! We must have looked ridiculous. Slimey was wearing a T-shirt and shorts (shorts! With his legs!) and Mum was wearing a horrible sort of boiler suit and looking really dumpy. Definitely middle-age spread. In addition to the shorts, Slime was humping an enormous backpack. You'd have thought he was going on a round-the-world hike. I wore jeans and was the only one who looked half-way normal.

It was a really draggy sort of day because all we did was walk on the Heath and occasionally sit down and eat stuff and then get up again and do more walking and then sit down again to have a drink, and then they wanted to read their Sunday papers, which actually was the best bit because it meant I could go off on my own, which I did, and met this girl throwing sticks for her dog. She let me join in, which was fun. It was a really good dog, a German shepherd, which I would love, but some hopes.

Anyway, after all that we got on the tube and came home again, and what was supposed to be the point of it is what I want to know? If they wanted to go for a walk and sit on the grass and eat things why not just go up the road to the Common? Why trail all the way to Hampstead Heath? Mum says it's because Slimey used to live there before he married Mum and moved in with us and made my life a misery. Well, she didn't say that bit. I said that bit. I will never accept him as a second dad.

Dad was supposed to ring me this evening but he must have been too busy. Mum has said I can go and stay with him at half term. A whole week! Hooray!

The food today was pretty horrific, incidentally, for a true carnivore such as myself. Vegetarian sausages, for heaven's sake! I just munched in glum silence, not saying anything, as I could tell that Mum was really enjoying herself and I didn't want to spoil things for her, but she needn't think I didn't notice because I most certainly did. And if she thinks I am going to become a cranky veggie, she has another thing coming!

I'm really looking forward to tomorrow because HE is going to be away. He's going to go and bore some poor little kids at a school in Newcastle, showing them pictures of elves. That means Mum and I will be on our own! Double hooray!

Monday

It's just as well I made things up with Skinny Melon today because it turns out she was 100% right. My worst fears have come true. Mum is going to have a baby.

She broke it to me after tea, just as I was thinking we could settle down to have a lovely evening all to ourselves like we used to before HE came. She said, "I know I should have told you months ago—" and then she didn't get any further because I said, "Months? You mean it's been going on for months?" and she admitted that it had. She said that she is going to have it, "Some time in the New Year... on or about St Valentine's Day." That is the 14th of February! No wonder she looks bulgy round the middle.

I hate Slimey Roland worse than ever now. Doing this to my mum! I bet it was his stupid idea. He's all gooey about babies. Mum would never have thought of it for herself. She and Dad were going to have another one once only she decided against it, so if she decided against it with Dad why would she go for it with Slime? She surely can't want to have a baby that's going to be all gingery and freckled and look like a fungus?

She kept trying to butter me up. Trying to make me feel better about it. She kept saying things like, "It'll make us a proper family", and "It'll be nice for you to have a brother or sister". I don't want a brother or sister! I hate babies! They mess themselves and yell all the time. They are totally disgusting. And its surname will be Butter and it'll belong to them, to Mum and him, and I'll be an outsider.

I'll never forgive him for this. Never!

Tuesday

I told Skinny Melon this morning that she was right, and she said, "Oh, you're so lucky! That is totally brilliant. I wish my mum would get married again so that we could have another baby."

There are times when I think that Skinny is not quite right in the head.

After school we had a rehearsal for the Christmas play and those of us that are angels were taught the angels' song. We each get to sing one verse on our own and then the chorus all together. Mr Freely came in while we were doing it and said, "My goodness, that is some voice Cherry has!" One or two of the others put their hands to their ears and complained that I was deafening them, but you have to sing loudly if people at the back are going to be able to hear you, and it is a rock nativity, after all. Not the wishy-washy churchy kind. That's why Miss Burgess chose me, because I have this big voice.

I really enjoy singing. It has made me wonder whether perhaps I ought to try and be a pop star when I'm older. I know it is an overcrowded profession and that last year I thought I might want to be a judge, but being a pop star would bring deep joy to a great many people's lives whereas quite often judges do the exact opposite.

This is me being a pop star

Oooh!!

This is me being a judge

Maybe I could be a judge after I've finished being a pop star as I don't think you can be a judge until you are quite old, by which time I would most likely be bored with the other. I once heard someone say that fame could become very wearisome.

Actually, the reason I would like to be a judge is so that I could say to children when their parents are trying to get divorced, "Do you want them to get divorced?" and if the children said no, then the parents wouldn't be able to do it.

I'd have said no. I didn't like Mum and Dad quarrelling but I hate having to live with Slimey Roland and Dad having another wife. What I'd have said is you've got to turn the house into flats, one upstairs and one downstairs, and Mum can live in one and Dad can live in the other and I could live in both of them and go upstairs or downstairs as I liked. That, I think, would be perfect.

Or else they could have sold the house and bought two littler ones next door to each other and knocked a hole through the middle. They could be in Southampton so that Dad could still do his new job. They could be in cottages with chimneys and little gardens.

And Dad could go off to work and Mum could stay at home and read her books and they wouldn't ever have to see each other if they didn't want, they could even go out with other people, I wouldn't mind, just so long as they came home at night and were always there.

I said all this to Skinny once and she said that if she had a dad she'd want him to live in the same house as her and her mum and her brother and sister and for them all to be together all of the time. This would be her idea of heaven.

I agree it would be mine if Dad could come back and he and Mum didn't quarrel.

There's a boy at school called Timothy Dunbar who lives with his mum during the week and his dad at weekends. He reckons it's brilliant as his dad spoils him rotten, giving him presents and taking him to places of interest, which he never did when he was at home. But it's all right for Timothy Dunbar. His dad only lives just a few streets away and his mum hasn't gone and got married again.

Slimey came back tonight. Worse luck. I was hoping he might have fallen through a crack in the paving stones.

Wednesday

Mouse droppings and jellied eyeballs. Or maybe it was frogspawn. Either way it was disgusting.

Now that Mum has told me about the baby she seems to think it's OK for her to keep on talking about it. She said to me at teatime, while Slime was upstairs with his elves, "What do you think we should call it? Think of some names!" I said, "There aren't many names that go with Butter." I said, "Barbara Butter, Brenda Butter, Belinda Butter," very heavily sarcastic, but that was the wrong thing as Mum immediately thought it meant that I was interested. She said, "Would you like it to be a girl?" Very quickly, and just as sarcastic, I said, "Bertram Butter, Bruce Butter, Bernard Butter." All Mum said was, "Bernard's nice! I like Bernard."

Bernard Butter? She has to be joking!

Slimey Roland brought me back a china figure from Newcastle. It is a Victorian lady with a crinoline and the crinoline is made of real lace.

My Victorian Lady →

Mum says it is valuable and that I must be careful not to break it. It is quite nice, I suppose. I have put it on the top shelf near my bed.

I would much rather have had a dog.

Thursday

I have found something new to worry about. Suppose Mum dies while she is having this baby? People do die. In olden times they were always dying in childbirth. Even today it could still happen. I couldn't sleep last night for thinking about it. It would be all Slimey's fault! Why couldn't he keep out of our lives? Why couldn't he leave Mum alone? We were perfectly happy without him!

Friday

I asked Mum two things when I got in from school and to both of them she said no.

First of all I asked her yet again if I could take sandwiches instead of having school dinner because today it was something quite unspeakable, I mean it looked as if it had been scraped up off the pavement. It is only a question of time before I get terminally poisoned. Mum said, "You can take sandwiches so long as you're prepared for them to be vegetarian" which as far as I'm concerned is the same as saying no because I am not going to change my eating habits just to please Slime. What's being veggie ever done for him? Made him look like a fungus. And anyway, it would mean he'd won and then he'd get all unbearable and triumphant.

So we had a bit of a dispute about it, with me saying why couldn't I have ham or chicken and Mum saying because it upsets Slime to see dead things in the fridge (and me thinking but not saying that it upsets me to see Slime in the house) and that if I choose to eat meat at school that's up to me but we're not going to have it at home, which means we shall all end up looking like fungus. Except by then I shall probably be dead of food poisoning so I suppose it really doesn't matter.

Anyhow, we then had tea and I said, "Oh, by the way, Gemma Parker has invited me to her sleep-over tomorrow. Is that OK?" and Mum tightened her lips and said, "Well, no, as a matter of fact I'm afraid I don't think it is. I think I'd rather that you stayed away from Gemma Parker."

I knew she'd say that. She has taken it into her head that Gemma is a bad influence all because last term she heard her say a four-letter word that she doesn't even know the meaning of. Gemma, that is. It was just something she'd heard her brother say. All the boys say it; all the older ones. Even Skinny's brother, who Mum thinks is such a "nice young man". They go round shouting it at each other. It doesn't mean anything. They think it makes them sound butch and grown-up.

I said to Mum, "Everybody else is going. I'll feel left out." She said, "Not everybody can be. There wouldn't be room for them." "Well, everyone who is anyone," I said. "The Melon, for instance. Her mum doesn't mind."

Mum likes the Melon. I thought it would sway her, but it didn't. After about ten minutes of arguing she said, "Look, I'm sorry, Cherry, but that is that. I do not want you going to the sleep-over." I shrieked "Why not? When the Melon is allowed to?" Mum said, "You don't have to shout at me. What Melanie's mother allows her to do is neither here nor there. She probably doesn't know that family as I do. I just don't trust them."

The only reason she says this is because Gemma's mum smokes cigarettes and she and Slimey think that anyone who smokes cigarettes is some kind of criminal and ought to be locked up, and also because Gemma's dad happens to work in a place called Franco's that once got raided by the police, which is hardly Gemma's dad's fault. He can't help where he works. What Mum doesn't understand is that Gemma is totally naive. She's like a six year old. Her mum won't even let her watch television without supervision in case she sees something she shouldn't.

I tried explaining this to Mum but she plainly didn't believe me. She said, "If you ask me, Gemma's mother is rather flighty."

What does she mean, flighty? Does she think she's a witch, or something?

Mum told me not to sulk. She said that to make up for not letting me go to the sleep-over, we'd all have a meal in the pizza place tomorrow night and then we'd go to the DVD shop and I could choose whatever film I wanted. That cheered me up a bit as I thought that I would get something really gross that they normally wouldn't let me have. But honestly, what does she think we do at sleep-overs? We don't do anything! Just sit and talk and try on each other's clothes and then tell scary stories in the dark. Gemma's such a baby she usually falls asleep.

I am going to get a really *gross* DVD.

The really **gross** DVD...

Saturday

I am seriously annoyed. They wouldn't let me have any of the films I wanted. Mum said I was just picking them to be awkward, because of her not letting me go to the sleep-over. She said if I couldn't choose something sensible, then she would have to choose for me. When I pointed out that she had promised me, she said, "Oh, now, Cherry, act your age! You know perfectly well there are limits."

She never said anything about limits. She said I could choose whatever I wanted.

"Anything sensible," she said.

They cheat all the time, grown-ups do.

So while I'm mooching about looking for something sensible, and doing my best to find one they'd loathe, she and Slimey are wandering over to the kids' section and mooning about amongst the Walt Disneys. Suddenly I hear Slimey cry, "Oh, look, Butterpat!" (I nearly died. The girl behind the counter had to put her hand over her mouth to stop from sniggering.) "Look, Butterpat! Look at this... Snow White!"

And Mum squeaks, "Ohh! Snow White!" in a silly little girly voice, and claps her hands. "I haven't seen that since I was younger than Cherry!"

Slimey says, "Me neither. It used to be my favourite film when I was five years old." And Mum says, "Oh, we've got to have it! Cherry, it's all right, we've found one… we're going to watch *Snow White*!"

Which we did, whether I liked it or not. Which for the most part I did *not*. I mean, it's kids' stuff. Mum and Slimey sat there on the sofa together going oooh and aaah and "Oh, I remember this bit!" "That bit always terrified me!" Having a right nostalgia binge.

Afterwards I rang Gemma's number and spoke to Skinny. I asked her how the sleep-over was going and she said they were watching *When Harry Met Sally*, which actually I have already seen, though I wouldn't have minded seeing it again. At least it would have been better than *Snow Soppy White*. I said, "I'm surprised Gemma's mum lets her watch that," remembering certain bits which I felt sure she wouldn't think suitable. Gemma's mum is really strict, in spite of being flighty and going round on broomsticks. Skinny said, "She's sitting there with her finger on the fast forward button in case of dirty bits, but she can't always get there in time!" and we both giggled.

When I went back in the lounge Mum said, "It's good to hear you sounding so cheerful." I just frowned and didn't say anything. That is the second time Mum has broken her promise.

Sunday

Dad rang this morning. He said he and Rosemary are really looking forward to having me at half-term although it is unfortunate that I won't be able to stay with them for the whole week as they are both working and cannot get more than a few days off. He said they are very disappointed about this but they are not free agents like Mum and Slimey. They can't just take time off whenever they feel like it.

I said that I understood and that it would be lovely to get away even just for a few days. Dad said, "Why? Are you fed up? You're sounding a bit fed up." So I told him about Mum breaking her promises, not letting me have a dog or choose a video, and Dad said, "Breaking a promise to a child is one of the worst things you can do," which I must say I heartily agree with.

He said, "I can't offer you a dog, but when you come to us you can watch whatever DVD you like, and that is a PROMISE." I said, "You mean it? Any DVD I like?" and he said, "Any DVD except *Snow White* and those dratted Dwarves." And I hadn't even told him that that was what Mum and Slimey made me watch! He said they kept pushing it at him in his local DVD shop, trying to make him take it.

"Don't," I said. "It's really yucky."

Dad said, "I won't, don't worry! I was taken to see it as a kid and had nightmares for months afterwards."

Nightmares? What on earth could he have had nightmares about? Dad must have been an extremely sensitive little boy.

When I told Mum about him and Rosemary not being able to get time off she gave this sort of sneer, with her lip hooped up, and said, "You amaze me!"

"It's because they both go out and do proper work," I said. "They can't just go taking days off whenever they want, like you can."

"Of course they can't," said Mum, all sarky and snide.

"Well, they can't," I said. "They do very important jobs."

"I don't call being a computer programmer all that important," said Mum. "Nor being an office manager," she added.

It's Rosemary who's the office manager, Dad who's the computer programmer. They both work in the same office, which is probably quite nice for them.

I said, "If it wasn't important, nobody would care if they took time off," and to my surprise old Slimey jumped in and agreed with me. He said, "She's absolutely right!" and I saw him give Mum this funny little frown. I don't know what he did that for, but anyhow it stopped her trying to tell me that Dad isn't important, which I really resent. He said, "The way I see it, everyone is important in his own way." To which Mum snapped, "Her!" being a bit of a feminist which actually I am as well. So then old Slime says, "His or her. I stand corrected," and goes on to say that he personally doesn't see why a person that sweeps the road, for instance, should be considered any less important than a prime minister, which is just stupid. Anybody could sweep the road. Not anybody could be prime minister. And not anybody could be a computer programmer, either, so sucks to Mum! She certainly couldn't be.

141 Arethusa Road
London W5

18 October

My dear Carol,

Well, I've done it! My secret is out. On the whole she has taken it very well; far better than I'd dared to hope. To begin with I could see she was a bit stunned – as she had every right to be – and a bit put out that I hadn't told her sooner, but I apologised for that and admitted that I was a coward, and I think she understood.

I was dreading that she would feel resentful and that we'd be in for an attack of the sulks, but the other day she was even suggesting names to me and was starting to sound enthusiastic! I realise now that I was wrong to keep it from her – Roly said all along that I was – but I'm hoping no real harm has been done. I am making sure that we spend some part of every day talking about the baby together, even if it's just five minutes, so that she will be made to feel a part of it and not left out in the cold.

I'm glad you've had a good week (meeting handsome Texans! You just watch it!) because after a bumpy start so have we. Roly went away to Newcastle for just one night and I missed him more than I could have thought possible, but it gave me the opportunity I needed to talk to Cherry and make my confession, and when he came back the next day he'd brought her the most truly beautiful china ornament that he found in an antique shop. I told him that it's far too valuable to give to a child, especially one as clumsy as Cherry, but he insisted that he had bought it for her and that she must have it. She mumbled her thanks – not quite as ungraciously as usual – and seemed reasonably pleased with it. She has put it away very carefully on a high shelf, but it's only a matter of time before it gets smashed to smithereens.

I sometimes wonder whether Roly is trying too hard. Might it not be better if he gave her tit for tat and treated her with the same contempt as she treats him? Unfortunately – or fortunately – it's just not in his nature. He is a very gentle, caring person and I'm afraid that a child like Cherry rides rough-shod over him. I'm hoping that the baby may bring out the softer side of her nature. If she has one!

No, that's not fair. She has on the whole a very sunny personality, very bright and bubbly, and can be quite warm and loving when she chooses. I remember after Gregg and I first split up she was incredibly supportive. I couldn't have asked for a better daughter! It's just that at the moment events are rather conspiring to bring out the worst.

On Saturday she wanted to go to something she calls a sleep-over at a friend's house and we had a bit of a scene when I wouldn't let her. Roly says I should have taken the chance, but he hasn't seen the parents!!! The father works in a gambling den and the mother – well! The mother is something else. Huge peroxide beehive, mascara ten inches thick, mock leopardskin coat. Roly says what does it matter, but I don't want Cherry being led into bad ways and coming back here using foul language, which she is likely to do. The child swears like a trooper. Anyway, to make up for not letting her go we all went up the road for a pizza and then came back to watch a DVD. Guess what we saw? SNOW WHITE! Did you ever see it when you were a kid? I adored it – and still do! Cherry was inclined to be rather sniffy at first but afterwards she went out into the hall to telephone one of her friends and I heard her laughing, so she was obviously happy, which is something she hasn't always been just lately.

She's desperately looking forward to staying with Gregg for a few days at half-term. I just hope he doesn't let her down. Originally she was going to go for the whole week, but surprise, surprise! He can't get the time off. Funny he could spend a whole fortnight in Florida back in July and is going off skiing for another fortnight at Christmas, but can't spare just one week to be with his own daughter.

I know I mustn't run her dad down in front of her, but the temptation is sometimes very strong! Happily on this occasion, bless him, Roly stepped in before I could open my big mouth and say something which I might afterwards have regretted. I wouldn't want to poison Cherry's mind against her dad. I won't say she regards him as a god, exactly, but he is certainly far higher in the popularity stakes than my poor Roly. On the other hand, I do believe I have detected a slight softening in her attitude just recently. I am keeping my fingers crossed!

Please report on handsome Texans.

Love from

Patsy

Monday

He's still shoving these stupid cards under my door. I really hate the thought of him creeping about doing that while I'm asleep. I just keep chucking them in the waste-paper basket. I'm still on strike and so the basket is practically overflowing and everything is thick dust except for the crinoline lady on her shelf. I am too scared to dust her because she is so fragile and so I blow on her, ever so gently. Maybe if she gets too dirty I can give her a bubble bath and use the hair dryer.

Terrible row with Mum this morning when I arrived downstairs in T-shirt and leggings and my Doc Marten's. She screamed, "You can't wear that gear to school! You go back upstairs and change immediately!" I said, "Into what?" I said, "It may have escaped your memory, but we don't happen to have any school uniform at this school, we can wear whatever we like, and right now everybody is wearing T-shirt and tights and Doc Marten's."

Mum said not to take that tone with her. (What tone? What is she talking about?) She said she didn't care what other people were wearing, she wasn't having her daughter go to school looking like some kind of big-footed grotesque. I said, "That is very big-footist." And she snarled, "Never mind the smart mouth! I have spoken and that is flat and final. How can you expect to do any serious learning in that ridiculous get-up?"

Mum is incredibly set in her ways. I said, "Well, if it comes to that, how can you expect to have any serious baby, wearing those ridiculous dungarees?" which is what she has taken to wearing now that her secret is out. I said, "I bet the Queen didn't wear dungarees when she was having babies." Mum started to get all red and hot, but old Slimey laughed and said, "She's got you there!" almost as if he were on my side against Mum. She still wouldn't budge.

I met the Skinbag at the school gates and asked her what the sleep-over was like. She said it was brilliant and that Harry meeting Sally was even better second time round and why wouldn't my mum let me go? I told her it was because of Gemma's brother saying That Word and Mum thinking I might start saying it and the Melon agreed that mothers could be a real drag. She said that right at this moment hers was being even more of a drag than usual which I found hard to believe as the Melon's mum is really nice. She would for instance never make promises and then break them. Like if she said the Melon could have a dog, then she'd let her have a dog. I mean she's already got one, of course, but if she'd said she could have another, or choose a video or whatever, she would let her. So I said, "How is she being a drag?" but the Melon wouldn't tell me. She just said, "Behaving like a teenager."

I don't see anything particularly draggy about that.

When I got home from school, Mum started on about the baby again, wondering whether it was going to be a boy or a girl, trying to get me to say which I'd prefer. I wouldn't prefer either! I don't want to know about the beastly baby. I hope it never comes out. I hope it withers on the vine. I hate it!

Tuesday

Boiled organs and baked toenails for dinner. It was one of the boys that said they were organs. Male organs. He fished some out and made rude patterns with them on the table. Boys like doing that kind of thing. Skinny said she thought the toenails might in fact be potato skins, but who wants to eat potato skins? What happened to the insides of the potatoes? Skinny says we'll probably get to have those tomorrow, all lumpy and foul.

Got into trouble with Mrs James today because she said I was rude to her. I wasn't! She accused me of passing notes and I wasn't passing notes, it was John Lloyd and Steven Carter, I just happened to pick one up off the floor for them. Mrs James said, "There are other ways of letting me know that you have been falsely accused. There is no need to be aggressive."

I complained to Skinny Melon about it afterwards and Skinny said, "Well, you were aggressive. You always are, these days. People hardly dare open their mouths in case you jump on them."

I can't help it. I feel aggressive. I feel like screaming, sometimes. It's living with Mum and Slimey and this baby that Mum's carting around with her. That's what's doing it.

I keep remembering when Dad was here, before he and Mum started having rows. I was happy then. I haven't been happy ever since Mum and Dad split up. I hate them all!

Wednesday

Got into more trouble. Miss Bradley, this time. We were playing netball and she pulled me up for running with the ball when I wasn't. She just thought I was because someone barged into me. I explained this to her, as polite as could be. I said, "Excuse me, but you have made a mistake," and she instantly leapt down my throat and yelled that she was sick and tired of what she called my "attitude", and that if there was any more of it I would be suspended from the team. Why does everyone keep getting at me all the time? I can't wait till it's half-term and I can go and stay with Dad!

I was so disgruntled, what with Miss Bradley having a go at me and Skinny and me being a bit distant after her telling me yesterday I was aggressive, that I decided I wasn't going to stay in at lunch-time like we're supposed to. For one thing I couldn't stand the thought of having to eat the insides of yesterday's potatoes, and for another, I saw Skinny going off with Avril Roper and Uchenna Jackson, so I hopped out through the gates when no one was looking and went into town. I got some crisps and a bottle of Coke and walked up the road to the station, which is where the cab company is that Dad used to work for after he'd been made redundant.

Lots of the same drivers were there and they remembered me and asked me how I was doing and how Dad was liking his new job. They're ever so much more fun than the people Mum and Slimey know. All of Mum and Slimey's friends are either writers or publishers or something else to do with books. Books are all they ever talk about. They're always pushing them at me.

"Here's a copy of my new book for you, Cherry." "Here's a copy of a book we've just published, Cherry." "Here's a copy of a book I thought you might like, Cherry."

And then I'm expected to sit down and read them and say what I think of them, which most of the time isn't much, only I'm not allowed to say so for fear of being thought rude or hurting their feelings. It's not that I don't like books, just that I don't like *their* books. The sort they push at me. They're all so babyish! I'm more into the hard stuff. Horror, and that. Mum and Slimey are horrified (ho ho!) but I say what's wrong with reading something a bit scary? They don't seem to realise that I've grown out of all this kiddy stuff.

Anyway, when it was time to go back to school one of the drivers, who is called Ivy, said she'd take me in her cab. We talked a bit on the way and Ivy asked me how I was getting on with my mum's new husband. I was glad she didn't say "your new dad" as I can't stand it when people do that. So I pulled a face, and Ivy said, "Tough going?" And then she told me how it had happened to her when she was about my age and how she'd thought she'd never get used to her mum having a new bloke, "Never!" but how in the end she had and, "Now we're the best of friends."

I know Ivy was only trying to be helpful, but I am afraid it is not going to work out like that for me. I still have my real dad, even if he does live miles away. It was different for Ivy as her real dad was not really a very nice person. In fact Ivy said he was "a right *******". (I have to put stars as the word Ivy used is not the sort of word I wish to record in this diary.) I told her that my dad is the best dad in the world and that I am going to stay with him over half-term. I said that I am really looking forward to it. Ivy said, "Well, have a good time, but don't expect too much, will you?"

I don't know why she said that. I didn't have a chance to ask her as we had already reached the school gates. Skinny was mooning about nearby with Avril and Uchenna. You should have seen their faces when they realised who was in the cab!

Skinny   Avril   Uchenna

They couldn't have been more surprised if I'd stepped out of a Rolls Royce. Skinny shrieked, "Where have you been?" It was just my bad luck that Mrs James happened to be passing at that particular moment and also wanted to know where I had been. I told her I'd been visiting my dad's old work-mates and she said, "You do know you're not supposed to leave the premises at lunch time without permission?" and I said yes, which was a dumb thing to say. I should have said no, though I don't expect ignorance is any defence, and she said, "Very well, Cherry," all frozen and unsmiling like an ice lolly with the colour sucked out of it.

Mrs James looking like an ice lolly!

I am to go and see her tomorrow, first thing after assembly.

I know what that means. It means she's going to bawl me out and threaten to tell Mum. I don't care! It was worth it. I'm glad I went. I don't see what right they have to keep making all these rules and regulations anyway. Nobody ever asks us what we want. Grown-ups do just whatever they like. Get divorced. Marry creeps. Have babies. It isn't fair!

Thursday

Went to see Mrs James. Actually she was quite nice. She said that "this sort of behaviour" couldn't be allowed to go on but that she didn't want to have to write to Mum unless I absolutely forced her, and then she said, "Did you ever think about my suggestion for keeping a diary?" and I said yes, I was doing it, and she asked me if it was helping, but without prying into the reasons why I might need helping, which is what lots of teachers would have done. So to please her I said I thought perhaps it was, just a little bit, and she told me to keep on with it because it could only be a good thing.

I hope she's right. I do quite like putting things down in writing. I can say lots of stuff that I couldn't say to anyone else, not even the Melon – who is back being friends with me again, incidentally. It seems that we can't survive without each other. Avril and Uchenna are all right, but me and Skin have been together since Juniors.

I stayed in school at lunch-time and dutifully ate yuck in the canteen. It made me feel sick. I feel sick most of the time now, what with eating yuck and Mum and Slimey keeping on and on about this blessed baby. Even the names they have come up with are yuck. If it's a boy it's going to be Bernard... Bernard Butter. If it's a girl it's going to be Belinda. Mum says she likes what she calls the allitration.

Alliteration. (Just looked it up in the dictionary.) This

means having two letters the same. B and B. Like bed and breakfast. Or bread and butter.

I have just thought of a joke. If it's a girl they could call it Bredan, which is Brenda mixed up. Ha ha! That is a Slimey joke. I shall suggest it to them.

Friday

Dog's vomit and earwax, with crusty bits on top. I didn't ask anyone what it was supposed to be. I think it's better not to know. I just held my breath and swallowed. I am seriously thinking of taking up Mum's offer of vegetarian sandwiches. I would if it weren't for him. Old Slimey. I hate the thought of him crowing because he's won me over. If I decide to do it, it will be out of sheer desperation and a desire not to be poisoned. Nothing whatsoever to do with him.

When I got in at tea-time he was there, which I didn't expect him to be as he'd gone off to bore some more poor little kids, showing them how he draws elves. So I told them my idea for calling the baby Bredan and Mum (stupid) said, "Oh, you mean like Bredon Hill? But that's pronounced Breedon." Slime got it. He got it straightaway. He said, "Bredan Butter! Brilliant!" and promptly started to sketch a loaf of bread on the kitchen table with his felt-tip pen that he always keeps handy in case sudden inspiration comes to him. Mum said, "Oh! Yes. I see. Then we'd have a Roll and

Butter and a Bread and Butter. Clever!"

Slimey said, "Yes, and if we had another we could call it Toastan." I have been trying without success to think of other things that go with butter. All I can think of is T.K. Cann-Butter and Chris P. Bredan Butter. But they are not very good.

I suppose you could have Saul T. Butter. That is not bad.

A woman over the road who has just moved in has asked Mum if I'd like to go and have tea tomorrow with her daughter because her daughter is the same age as me and doesn't yet know anyone. Mum has gone and said that I will! It is terrible the way grown-ups just dispose of one's life for one. I don't particularly want to go and have tea with this person's daughter. She is called Sereena, which I know is not her fault, and her surname is Swaddle, which again I know she cannot be blamed for. Sereena Swaddle. That is alliteration. Mum says it is "unfortunate", but why she should think it's any more unfortunate than Belinda or Bernard Butter is beyond me.

Skinny rang later to know if I wanted to go swimming with her tomorrow afternoon and I had to say that I was having tea with this Sereena person. Skinny said "Who?" and I said, "Sereena Swaddle," and she said, "You're joking!" I said that I only wished I was. I went back to Mum and said, "Do I have to do this thing?" and she said, "Oh, Cherry, just once! It won't hurt you. She's a sweet little thing, I know you'll like her."

When Mum said, "sweet little thing" old Slime caught my eye and pulled a face. I'd gone and pulled one back before I could stop myself. I don't think I ought to do that. It's like him and me being ganged up together against Mum. Mum must have sensed it because she said, "You can laugh! It's nice to know there still are some sweet little things… they don't all clump around in bovver boots shouting four-letter words and watching ghastly horror movies."

I have just thought of something else that could go with butter. P. Nutt-Butter. That is a good one!

Saturday

Ha! So much for Mum not letting me go to Gemma's sleep-over in case she corrupted me. I went to have tea with the Sereena person this afternoon. The sweet little thing who doesn't swear or watch horror movies. I can see why Mum thought she was a sweet little thing. It is because she has a sweet little face. (Yuck!) She also has long blonde hair and rose-pink cheeks and eyes the size of satellite dishes and blue as whatever's blue. The sky. Forget-me-nots. Saffires. Rather revolting, really. At least, I think so. But it's what grown-ups like.

So anyway, we had tea and her mum was there and she's sort of… frothy. All fizzing and bubbling like Andrew's Fruit Salts that Dad used to take for his acid

Sereena ↑

indigestion. She kept giggling and saying things like, "Oh, Reena." (That's what she calls her. Double yuck.) "Oh, Reena, isn't this fun! You've found a friend already!" But I don't know whether I want to be her friend. I like to choose my own friends, and besides, I've got Skinny.

Afterwards we went up to her room and she said, "What do you want to do?" And I said, "Whatever you want to do." And she said, "Would you like to see some pictures of people having babies?"

I said, "I've seen pictures of people having babies. We did all that in Juniors."

"All right," she says. "What about pictures of people completely starkers?" I said, "Where would you get pictures of people starkers?" and she said her best friend Sharon where she used to live had torn them out of a magazine and photocopied them for her. She said some of them were really gross. Do you want to have a look?"

I was tempted to say yes as I thought it would pay

88

Mum out for not letting me go to Gemma's sleep-over, and also it would be a new experience and I do believe in having new experiences, but really to be honest I didn't fancy it, I mean that sort of thing could put you off for life and I would like to grow up to be reasonably normal.

Sereena said, "Oh, well, if you don't think you can take it, I'll tell you some jokes instead, shall I?" And before I can stop her she's telling me all these jokes that her friend Sharon had told her and which I shall not repeat in here as this is a diary and not a reseptikle for filth.

Pause while I look in the dictionary. That word is spelt receptacle. And saffire is spelt sapphire. I am very good at spelling, on the whole. Mrs James said to me the other day (before we had our little talk), "Your spelling and punctuation are excellent, Cherry." On the other hand I cannot understand figures, which is what Mr Fisher, who takes us for maths, calls "a decided drawback". Mum can't understand figures either, and nor can Slimey Roland, but it doesn't matter to them as they do the sort of jobs where figures are not important. Mr Fisher says that anyone who is not numerate, meaning anyone that can't add up or subtract, will have a hard time of it in the 21st century. He says we must come to terms with technology or perish.

Computers are technology and I'm not very good with computers, either. I don't know what I will end up

Me in ↑
the future

doing. Sweeping the streets, I expect. I don't think I
will be able to work with books like Mum, as I don't
think there will be any real books left. And I don't
think there will be people drawing pictures of elves,
either. It will all be done by computer and people such
as myself will be left behind like old empty bottles on
the beach.

I tried talking about this with Sereena, thinking I would
find out what kind of things she is good at other than telling
rude jokes, but you cannot have a proper conversation with
her as you can with the Melon. All she can do is bat her

satellite dishes and giggle. Of course the Melon is a bit of an intellectual, I mean, she has a real brain. Sereena's brain if she has one, is about the size of a pea.

When I got home Mum said, "There! That wasn't so bad, was it?" I told her it was "enlightening" and she said, "Why? What did you do?" I said, "Read porno mags and told dirty jokes." Mum laughed. She thought it really funny. "No, seriously," she said.

I said that seriously we had discussed what we thought would happen in the 21st century and I had come to the melancholy conclusion that far from being a pop star or a judge I would most likely end up living in a cardboard box as I was not numerate and couldn't make friends with computers the way some people could. Skinny, for example, and Sereena. Mum told me not to be so pessimistic. She said, "You're like me, you're into words." I said yes, but there won't be any words. Just computerspeak. Mum said, "Oh, what a bleak picture!" I said, "Yes, it is, but I think one has to face facts."

Mum doesn't want to face them. She says that if it's going to be a world without books and pictures then she'd sooner not be here. Slimey didn't play any part in this conversation as he was upstairs finishing some more elves to meet what is called "a deadline", meaning (I think) that his publishers will sue him for vast sums of money if he hasn't drawn the right number by a certain date.

It was nice being on my own with Mum, even if our conversation was rather doom-laden. At least she didn't mention the baby, which is now sticking out in front of her like a huge horrible sack of potatoes.

She asked me the other day if I'd like to feel it but I said no, thank you very much. Catch me!

Tomorrow I am going to stay with Dad. Hooray hooray hooray! Three whole days without Slimey Roland! No more stupid jokes, no more stupid cards! I can go to bed at night and know that nobody is going to come creeping along the passage and shoving stuff under my door while I'm asleep, which is something I really hate.

Dad is picking me up in the car. He is driving all the way from Southampton and is arriving at about 9 o'clock, so I must be sure and be up early. I am going to set my alarm. Fortunately I have already packed my case, I did it this morning with Mum's help. She kept saying things like, "Well, you won't need all that much, now it's only for a few days." She just refuses to accept that Dad is an important person and cannot simply please himself. This is because he is in an office. All Mum and Slimey ever do is sit at home reading books and drawing elves. But with Dad, there is a great deal depending on him and he has to be prepared to work long hours. It is not his fault. I do wish Mum could see this.

I am going to take my diary with me just in case, but I expect I shall be too busy to write anything in it. The next three days are going to be ACTION PACKED!!!

Dearest Carol,

I cannot believe it! A Texan called <u>Dwayn</u>? Is this a real name??? He sure does sound hunky, hon!

No, no, no, I'm only joking! In all seriousness, I'm really glad you've found someone to have fun with. You deserve it. Enjoy! But full reports, please. I am consumed with vulgar curiosity.

Cherry has suggested that if the baby is a girl we should call her Bredan…get it? Oh, ho ho! She is picking up this sort of humour from Roly. But I was so pleased that she feels able to make jokes about it. It shows she's been thinking.

Yesterday she went over the road to have tea with a new little girl who has just moved into our neighbourhood. I call her a little girl because although she is the same age as Cherry she is most delightfully quaint and old-fashioned! She actually wears a big red bow in her hair and shiny shoes with ankle straps. It takes me right back! Cherry by contrast is into all this heavy grunge gear and walks around looking like something that's crawled out of a garbage heap. I feel it would do her good to make friends with someone like little Sereena.

At the moment she is not here as she has gone off to spend a few days with Gregg. There are times when I could cheerfully strangle that man! He had arranged to pick her up at about nine o'clock and she was all ready and waiting, down in the hall with her suitcase, wearing her best clothes (ie, the grungiest ones she could find) and by 10.30 when he still hadn't arrived I rang Southampton and got this bimbo he's shacked up with and she says, "Oh, yah, he's just left about ten minutes ago." Of course by then the roads were busy which meant he didn't get here until lunch-time.

It really is too bad. Poor little Cherry sitting there waiting like some faithful hound, and this selfish irresponsible oaf not even bothering to call and let us know! Cherry was almost in tears. When he finally turned up she went catapulting into his arms and it was all kissy kissy huggy huggy. I expect I ought to have found it touching but the truth is I was too cross. Also, I suppose, if I am to be honest, I was a bit hurt at her being so obviously eager to get away from us. Roly says, "Come on, it's her dad! She hasn't seen him for six months," and I know that I mustn't be jealous but it seems so unfair! He comes breezing in, three hours late, and she's all over him with never so much as a backward glance for me and Roly. I offered the fool a cup of coffee (I wasn't going to offer him lunch!) but I could tell that Cherry just wanted to be off.

Oh, aren't I sour and crabby! But I do dread her returning home full of discontent, telling me how wonderful it is at her dad's and how horrible it is here. They're bound to spoil her rotten, it's only to be expected. And it will never occur to her that they've only had her for three days while we have her all the rest of the year! She's a bright child, but not always the easiest, which I know is partly my fault. My fault and Gregg's. Our getting divorced has been difficult for her. I keep telling myself that I must make allowances.

Oh, but she can be so ungracious! Roly felt that he would like to give her something as a going-away present. A little something to take with her. He said would she like a book and I said yes, I thought a book would be an excellent idea, because one thing she does do is read, even if it is mostly schlock horror just at present. He went to such pains to find one that she would like! She is writing this diary at the moment (it is supposed to be a secret, but she lets slip these little remarks from time to time) and we suddenly remembered that wonderful book which you and I read when we were Cherry's age. *I Capture the Castle*. Do you remember it? Cassandra Morton sitting on the draining board writing her journal with her feet in the sink? How we wallowed in it! So Roly combed through half the secondhand bookshops in London until he found an actual original copy and he slipped it into her bedroom while she was asleep, with one of his lovely funny little notes all done in pictures, telling her to take it with her to read while she was away, and what do you think? I've just been in there (it looks like a bomb site but I am not going to clear it) and she has just left the book lying on the floor! I haven't dared to tell Roly, he would be so hurt.

I really do begin to despair. It sometimes seems to me that the harder Roly tries the worse she treats him. And I have this horrible feeling that she is going to be even more impossible when she comes back from Gregg's.

Children! Think twice before embarking, no matter how handsome your Texan may be!

Eagerly await news of developments from your end. Will report back from mine.

Love from

Patsy

PS We are going to take the opportunity to re-decorate the spare bedroom ready for the baby while Cherry is away. We are also going to go and buy all the necessary paraphernalia – prams, potties, nappies! I thought I'd finished with all that. Roly is really excited. I only wish Cherry were, so that we could share it. I could really look forward to the event if I thought that she were happy.

Monday

No time to write in here yesterday so I am doing it now while Rosemary has her bath and gets ready to go out. She takes a long time to get ready, at least she did yesterday when we went for a pizza. We are going to go out every single day that I am here! This is because Rosemary doesn't like cooking, which is all right by me. I like to go out.

Tonight we are going for an Indian meal and tomorrow we are going for a Chinese one. To think that at home we only go out about once every six months! But Dad and Rosemary both do proper jobs and so I expect they earn a lot more money than Mum and Slimey, which is only right. Just sitting about reading books and drawing elves can't be classed as proper jobs. I don't think so.

I have only met Rosemary two times before so that I do not really know her very well. The times that I have met her are once before she got married to Dad (they did it in a love temple in the Seychelles. Incredibly r-r-r-romantic!) and once after, when they came back. That was almost a year ago. Since then I have only seen Dad in London except once when I came to Southampton just for the day and Rosemary was not there.

She is quite pretty and wears lots of make-up and really smart clothes. She is younger than Mum and of course much slimmer. Even if Mum weren't having this baby she would still be much slimmer. She and Dad go jogging every morning and Rosemary also does aerobics. Dad has started to play squash and is not anywhere near as pudgy as when he was driving the cab.

It is I must say a great relief to be in a house – well, a flat actually – where everything isn't being got ready for a baby. There are no signs of a baby in this place, thank goodness!

It was strange at first being in a flat after being used to a house but now I think that I prefer it. I think it would be sensible if everyone lived in flats because then there would be a lot more land where you could grow grass and trees. I think probably it is almost antisocial for people to live in houses. I am going to say this to Slimey next time he starts on about the environment and how we are ruining it. Dad and Rosemary aren't taking up half the space that he and Mum take up! Also I enjoy everything being on one level so that you don't have to keep rushing up and down the stairs all the time. Also there is a lift, in which you can meet people and talk. I shall live in a flat when I am grown-up – if I am not living in a cardboard box, that is.

I told Dad about the cardboard box and he said that he will buy me a computer for my Christmas present. He said, "I cannot have a daughter of mine being computer-illiterate, but of course your mother has always had a tendency to be a bit of a Luddite." I said what was a Luddite and he said they were people who went round smashing machinery. I said that I didn't think Mum smashed it on purpose, she just wasn't very good with it, like for instance last week she broke the handle off the washing machine and put the vacuum bag in the wrong way so that all the dust came flying out into the house.

Dad said, "Typical! And I suppose he's not much better?" I said, "Slimey? He's even worse!" which isn't strictly speaking true since it was Slimey who fixed the handle of the washing machine with superglue and changed the bag in the vacuum cleaner. But it's true that neither of them knows the first thing about computers. Mum just uses her word processor like an ordinary typewriter, which was a thing that used to drive Dad mad when he was living with us. He was always trying to teach her different things that she could do with it and she wouldn't listen. She used to say, "Oh, I can't be bothered with all that!" Deliberate stupidity, Dad said it was.

The journey from London to Southampton in Dad's car was brilliant except that half-way here I started to feel sick, which Dad said was probably because I'd got out of the habit of travelling by car. I said yes, Slimey always insisted on going everywhere by bus or bicycle and Dad said the man was an idiot. He said, "Like it or not, the car is here to stay," and, "You can't put the clock back." Anyway, we had to stop a couple of times so that I could get some air and then I felt all right again. But I have never felt car sick before. It is all Slimey's fault.

Today we went for a drive to the New Forest (I didn't

get sick this time) and had lunch in a pub, in the garden, and then drove to a place called Lymington, which is at the sea, but it was too cold to go swimming and so we just looked at it and came home again. Tomorrow Dad has to go into the office in the morning because there is a problem which only he can sort out, so Rosemary and I are going to meet him for lunch and then go round Southampton where there are some things to be seen, such as an old museum and an ancient wall. Also of course the docks. I am looking forward to it.

I rang Mum last night to tell her that we had arrived safely as she worries about accidents, and she said, "So how are you getting on? I suppose everything is lovely?" I said that it was and that so far I was really enjoying myself (though in fact we hadn't done very much at that stage). I said, "Dad's told me I can stay till Friday if I want." He told me in the car. It was one of the first things he said. He said, "Rosemary's managed to wangle an extra two days and I'll take off what time I can."

"That's good, isn't it?" I said to Mum. I thought she would be pleased but she didn't sound very pleased. She just grunted and said, "If that's what you want."

"Well, I thought I might as well," I said. "Now that I'm here."

"That's right," said Mum. "Make the most of it. It doesn't happen that often."

Then there was a pause and she said, "You left your book behind." I couldn't think what she was talking about. I said, "What book?" She said, "Roly's book. The one he bought specially for you." I knew from the tone of her voice that she was mad at me. I forgot all about his stupid book! I wouldn't have brought it anyway. What do I want a book for, when I'm with Dad?

Mum said, "You're not worth giving things to, are you?" I am if they're the right things, but anyway she needn't go getting all wound up about it because I am also pretty wound up, if she wants to know. What I am wound up about is the thought of him actually opening my door and creeping into my room while I'm asleep. I don't think he has any right to do that. He's not my dad. But if I'd said so to Mum she'd only have got all defensive, like she always does where Slimey is concerned, and I didn't want to quarrel with her over the telephone. So I just said, "Look, I'm sorry, I forgot," and she said, "Yes, of course, you left in such a rush!" I think she was being sarcastic. It was the way she used to get with Dad when they were having words. I hope she's not going to start on at me. It's ever so nice and peaceful here. I don't want Mum ringing up and making trouble.

Tuesday

The museum was very interesting. It is called The Wool House and is all full of relics from Napoleonic days. French prisoners were kept there and you can still see their initials where they'd carved them into the wooden beams. It gave me a strange feeling to think of them doing that all those years ago and me standing here today looking at them. It made me wonder if people in two hundred years' time would stand and look at something I'd done, like for instance I once carved my initials on a tree and put the date. I imagined a girl like me finding it and wondering who I was and what had become of me. It was a bit creepy but at the same time comforting, to know that you have made your mark and will leave something behind you.

Tomorrow we are going to Portsmouth to see the *Victory*, which is the ship that Nelson sailed in.

Wednesday

We couldn't go to Portsmouth today because Dad was needed at the office again. Well, Rosemary and I could have gone but it wouldn't have been the same without Dad. She said we could go if I liked, but I said I'd rather wait for him and she said she would, too. She said as a matter of fact there were things she had to do, like finishing off an evening dress she is making for herself for a very posh dinner party that she and Dad are going to on Friday night. She said would I mind terribly if she stayed in and did that?

Of course I said no and she said I could do whatever I

wanted, watch the television or go for a walk. She said there was a park just up the road, so I went up there but it wasn't very interesting, no dogs to play with and nothing really to do, so I came back again and watched for a bit as she used her sewing machine and wondered why Mum couldn't make her own clothes. Mum is absolutely useless, she can't even sew on buttons properly. I also wondered why Mum couldn't wear the sort of clothes that Rosemary wears. Her evening dress, for instance, is completely incredible, off the shoulder and showing lots of bosom.

← Rosemary in her dress

I have never ever seen Mum wearing anything like that.

We were supposed to be meeting Dad again for lunch but he rang to say he wasn't going to be able to make it (some very important Americans have come over and he has to be with them). I could see that Rosemary was a bit put out by this. I think she didn't quite know what to do with me. She said, "I guess we'd better find some way of amusing you. There's a zoo over on the Common. Would you like to go to the zoo?" I said that I was very sorry but I didn't believe in zoos, I think it is cruel keeping animals locked up in small spaces, and she said, "Oh, you're one of those, are you? I'm surprised you're not a veggie." I said, "I probably am going to be, soon," and she pulled a face as if I'd announced that I was going to have all my teeth pulled out or my hands chopped off.

Since I wouldn't go to the zoo she suggested the cinema. She said, "There's bound to be something suitable for children, seeing as it's half-term." I told her that I didn't normally watch things that were suitable for children. She said, "Well, I'm not taking you to some ghastly horror movie, if that's what you're after." I said she didn't need to take me anywhere, I am quite accustomed to entertaining myself, and so we ate some soup and a tin of peaches in the kitchen and she went back to her evening dress and I came in here to write this diary.

It's now three o'clock and Dad still isn't back. Rosemary thinks probably he won't be back until about seven, when we can all go out for a meal. It's difficult thinking what to do until then. I don't really want to watch television because it's in the same room where she's doing her sewing and she's got the radio on. I've looked for some books but there don't seem to be any. I should have brought the one that Slimey got for me, but how was I to know that Dad would have to work?

Maybe I could go into Southampton and buy something.

Thursday

I don't think Rosemary will ever have a baby. I don't think she likes children very much. I said to her yesterday that I was going to go into Southampton to look round the shops and she said, "You can't go by yourself, you'll get lost." And then she heaved this big irritable sort of sigh and said, "I suppose I shall have to come with you." We couldn't go by car because Dad had taken it and so we had to go by bus, which is a thing I am quite used to on account of Slimey not driving but which I don't think she is as she kept tapping her foot and looking at her watch and trying to find out from the timetable when the next one was due. It made me feel guilty, as if I ought to have stayed quietly indoors, but it's just as well I didn't as Dad didn't get home until almost nine o'clock, by which time I had read two horror books (*Scream and You're Dead* and *House of Horror*) and was absolutely starving.

Today was better as we went to Portsmouth to see the *Victory*. Dad and I went; Rosemary didn't come. The *Victory* was very interesting and it was nice being with Dad on my own. He was more like I remember him from the old days. When he is with Rosemary he is different. It is hard to describe it but he is not like my dad. He is more like one of those men that drive round in fast cars with pony tails and telephones. What Mum and Slimey call yuppies.

When we got back from Portsmouth, Dad said I could go to the DVD shop and make my choice, as he had promised me. I was tempted to choose a horror film, just to show Rosemary that if I wanted to watch it I could, but then I thought maybe if I chose that Dad would be like Mum and break his promise and so I chose instead a film called *Strictly Ballroom* which is all about ballroom dancing which to be honest I am not really into but Skinny Melon had told me it had this really gorgeous-looking boy in it, and she was right, it did! He's heaven. I am now seriously thinking of asking Mum if I can learn ballroom dancing. Imagine meeting a boy like that! (Some hopes!)

Dad and Rosemary, unfortunately, got bored. Rosemary went and sat over the other side of the room and switched on a light and did her sewing, and Dad went off to have a bath, so that I was left on my own. I didn't really mind, I suppose, though it is nicer when other people enjoy what you enjoy. I think Mum would enjoy it. It is her sort of thing. Next time we get a DVD I shall tell her to get that one.

Tomorrow I am going home. I am trying to remember the things that I have seen and done so that I can tell Mum. I have been to the New Forest. I have been to the sea. I have been in the museum. I have seen the *Victory*. I have seen *Strictly Ballroom*. I have eaten: one Italian meal, one Indian meal, one Chinese meal, one French meal, and one American meal (hamburgers, only I had a vegeburger thinking of Slimey and dead things in the fridge). I suppose that is quite a lot of things to have seen and done in five days.

Later

Dad and Rosemary have just had a bit of an argument about which of them is going to drive me back tomorrow. I heard them when I went to the bathroom. (I have noticed, in a flat, you can quite often hear people talking. It is not as private as in a house.) I heard Rosemary say, "She's your daughter!" and then Dad said something that I couldn't catch but I think it was something about needing to go into the office again, and Rosemary said, "I am not driving her all the way to London and that is that!"

I'm glad she isn't driving me. I don't think I could bear it, and I don't expect she could, either.

Friday

Now I am back home. I had to come by train because of Rosemary refusing to drive me and Dad having to go into the office. It is a bit of a drawback in some ways having a father who is so important. I mean, I am glad of course that he is important, but I would have liked it better if he had been there more of the time as it was not so much fun when he wasn't. I don't feel very comfortable with Rosemary. I think she would rather I hadn't come.

I rang Mum before we left, to tell her what time my train was getting in. She was furious, I could tell. She said, "Train? All by yourself?" And I said yes, because Dad had to work. "Oh, does he?" she said. "Where is he? Let me speak to him!" I didn't want her to but she started to shout. She shouted, "You put him on the telephone!" It was so loud that Dad heard it and came and took the receiver off me. He said, "Hello? Pat?" quite pleasantly, I thought, but it soon developed into one of their rows.

I think Mum must have asked him why I couldn't stay till Saturday and come back by car because Dad sort of twisted his lips in a way which said, "I am being very patient but do not try me too far," and informed her that, "Rosemary and I happen to have a very important dinner party that we have to go to this evening. It is not something we can get out of, nor would we wish to. All right?"

I don't know what Mum said after that because I couldn't bear to listen any more. Why does everything always get so horrible when Mum and Dad talk to each other? I wish they hadn't! It ruined the end of my holiday.

Dad and Rosemary both came to the station with me. I would rather it had just been Dad, but at least

Rosemary stayed in the car which meant I was able to say goodbye to Dad on my own. He said, "We've had fun this week, haven't we? We must do it again – and not leave it so long next time." I said that maybe I could come at Christmas but Dad said unfortunately that wouldn't be possible as he and Rosemary had already arranged to go with some friends to Austria and do some skiing. I didn't like to suggest that maybe I could go with them as I don't think Rosemary would be happy. I don't think she likes me very much. So then I had a bright idea and said, "Parents' Evening! You could come to Parents' Evening!" Dad said he thought that was an excellent suggestion and if I let him know when it was, he would definitely be there. He said, "That's a promise!"

We had a bit of time to wait so we went over to the bookstall and Dad bought me some magazines and another horror book. Unlike Mum and Slimey, he didn't go "tut tut" about me reading horrors but said they looked jolly good and really exciting and ought to keep me on the edge of my seat all the way to London. As it happens I cannot read very well on trains as they jerk up and down and make my eyes go funny but I didn't say so to Dad. Instead I said that I would find out the date of Parents' Evening and let him know. He said, "Make sure you do!" and then it was time to say goodbye and for me to get on the train.

This was the first time that I have ever been on a long

train journey by myself. I kept worrying how I would know when we reached London, which was stupid because London is where the train stops. It doesn't go anywhere else. And then I worried about leaving my seat to go to the toilet in case I couldn't find my way back or someone stole my things. And then when I absolutely had to go because otherwise I would have to burst it was one of those ones where you have to press buttons to get in and more buttons to close the door and I was terrified I wouldn't be able to get out again, but of course I did. I expect if I got used to travelling on my own it would be all right.

Another thing I worried about was what I would do if I got to London and couldn't see Mum or Slimey, but Slimey was there, waiting for me, looking all Slimey-ish in an anorak and joggers and tatty old trainers.

He gave me a big hug and a kiss and I let him, which normally I wouldn't have done because normally it would revolt me, but I was

↑ Roly at the station

just so relieved to see him. He said, "I'm sorry Butterpat couldn't come, but she has an appointment at the clinic." (Meaning the ante-natal clinic, where all the pregnant women go to make sure they are having proper babies and not babies that have things wrong with them.) He said he knew that he was second best but, "Hopefully better than nothing."

I felt sort of sorry for him when he said this. I also felt a bit mean about leaving his book behind, especially as I was clutching my horror book. I explained that Dad had bought me the book and that I hadn't left his one behind on purpose, I'd simply forgotten to pack it, like I'd also forgotten to pack my tooth brush (this was a fib but I said it to make him feel better). I said that I wished I had taken his book as I'd had to go out and buy myself some, and I promised that I would read his next. Slimey said, "I'm afraid you won't find it very exciting after your diet of horror. I probably made a mistake in choosing it." He sounded really sad, as if it mattered to him that I mightn't find his book exciting. I said that I would definitely read it and let him know.

When we got home Mum was there. I'd forgotten how enormous she looks after Rosemary. She asked me if I'd had a good time and I said, "Brilliant," because it would have been disloyal to Dad to have said anything else. Mum said, "Well, there's nothing very brilliant on offer at this end, but we can go up to the DVD shop and get a DVD, if you like." I said, "Can I choose?" and Mum said, "Yes, but you know the rules." So I chose *Strictly Ballroom* and I was right, Mum loved it! So did Slime. Mum said it was a "good old-fashioned movie with no sex and no violence" and Slime surprised everyone – well, he surprised me, but I think Mum as well – by saying that he used to be a champion tango dancer, and to prove it he jumped up and pulled me into the middle of the room and taught me how to do it! He was really good. And so now I know how to tango!

me and Roly tango!

Saturday

He's still shoving cards under my door and I still don't like it but I suppose he is only doing it to try and be friendly. It is rather pathetic, really. Imagine being so desperate to be liked!

After breakfast I rang the Melon and we arranged to meet at the top of my road and go round the shops together. She wanted to know what it was like at Dad's so I said the same as I said to Mum, that it was brilliant. I told her all the things I'd done and then asked her what she'd done.

Skinny said she hadn't done anything at all. She sounded a bit down in the dumps so I asked her what the matter was and at first she said nothing was the matter but then she said that her mum had met this man at the place where she works and he was called Melvyn and he was dire. I was going to say that he couldn't possibly be any more dire than Slime but then for some reason I didn't. I don't know why. I said, "Maybe she just has bad taste in men but it doesn't really matter so long as she's not going to marry him." Skinny said rather fiercely that of course she wasn't going to marry him, he was just a boyfriend. I said, "So what's the problem?" and she said there wasn't one except that she couldn't stand the sight of him. Then she cheered up and said she wanted to go and buy a new pair of leggings with some money that he'd given her. I said, "Dire Melvyn?" and she giggled and said, "He's trying to worm his way into my good books!"

I really don't know what she's got to complain about.

When I got home I found that Slime had finished the pond. I have to say that it is quite nice. It will be very pretty in summer, with water lilies and bullrushes. It is not quite ready for the fish but next week we are going to go and buy some. I am refusing to be too enthusiastic because if I am it will make Mum think I have forgiven her for breaking her promise about the dog, which I most certainly have not.

I would still like a dog more than anything else in the world. Far more than a computer, though naturally I wouldn't say this to Dad. A computer will help me not to end up living in a cardboard box (maybe – maybe not) but a dog would bring immense cheer and comfort into my gloomy life. I could play with it and take it for walks and feed it and brush it and cuddle it and talk to it and it could even sleep in bed with me. Oh, why can't I have one? Trust Slimey Roland to go and suffer from stupid allergies!

My dear Carol,

Your Texan sounds more divine every time you
write! Photo, please. I picture him as being a sort of
cross between Steve McQueen and the Incredible
Hulk…my poor Roly cannot even begin to compete
but I don't care! I love him to death!

Well, Cherry has come back from Southampton and
just as I feared, they have spoilt her rotten. She
informs me that, "Dad took me out to dinner every
single night." Dad took her to have an Indian meal,
Dad took her to have a Chinese meal, Dad took her
to have a pizza, Dad took her to have oysters and
champagne (so she says), Dad took her to see the
Victory, Dad took her to the New Forest. I swear I
shall scream if she tells me once more of the
wonderful time she had with Dad!

Dad is a rat. He obviously had a guilty conscience
because when she got there he informed her that she
could stay on till Friday, but then I got a call early
Friday morning saying that he was sending her home
by train as he had to go into the office. When I asked

why she couldn't stay over until Saturday he had the nerve to tell me that he and this bimbo he's married are going to a dinner party – a dinner party, my dear! – which they certainly didn't intend to cancel just on Cherry's behalf. So she ended up being bundled on to the train like an unwanted parcel and shunted back to us. Of course that isn't the way she sees it. She just thinks that Gregg is enormously important and that the office can't function without him. All he is is a computer programmer!

According to Cherry he has promised to buy her a computer for Christmas, but I shall believe that when I see it.

I suppose it's being over-protective to worry about an eleven-year-old girl travelling on a train all by herself from Southampton to Waterloo, but I kept having these horrific visions of all the things that could possibly happen to her. A mother's mind is like a museum of horrors… I had to send Roly off to meet her as I was due at the clinic. He tells me she was quite jaunty, in fact her normal ebullient self, so she obviously didn't suffer. I was the one to do that!

I asked after the bimbo, hoping to hear how ugly/stupid/fat/useless/generally disagreeable she was but it appears that she's thin as a rake, ravishingly beautiful, dresses like a fashion model, makes all her own clothes, and is a hard-headed career woman. This, at least, is what I gather. What Cherry actually said, in scathing tones, was, "She's never likely to have a baby," which is simply a not very subtle way of having a go at me. I suppose she blames the baby for me not going to meet her off the train. It wouldn't occur to her to blame Gregg for putting her on the train in the first place!

Oh, what a moaning minnie I have become! I don't mean to be but there's only three months to go and she still shows no real signs of any softening in her attitude. I tried to show her what we'd done in the spare bedroom, but she made it very plain she didn't want to know. She is so full of "Dad" and what it's like at Dad's place – she even had a go at Roly today for living in a house and not a flat! It seems it is now environmentally irresponsible to live in a house. Dad could live in one if he wanted, he is so rich and important he could live anywhere, but he chooses to live in a flat so as not to waste land.

If you believe that, you'll believe anything! I don't know how Roly puts up with her. He has the patience of a saint.

Lots of love from your harassed,

Patsy

Sunday

Mum showed me today what they've done to the spare bedroom while I've been away. I was quite surprised! The walls are dead white with little figures running all the way round and in the middle lots of teddy bears and beach balls and space rockets have been painted. Oh, and elves, of course! Elves all over the place.

Roly's soppy paintings

Mum said, "What do you think?" and I said, "I don't remember having this when I was a baby," meaning it was really nice and the sort of thing that a baby would like, but Mum took it the wrong way and snapped, "That's because you weren't lucky enough to have Roly for a father!"

She is really touchy these days. I can't seem to do anything right.

Monday

I said to Skinny Melon today that I didn't think my system could stand much more poisoning from school dinners. She said she didn't think hers could, either. She said she was absolutely positive that the other day she'd found a bit of worm on her plate. She'd shown it to Mrs James (this was the day I bunked off and came back to school by cab) and Mrs James had looked at it and told her not to be silly, it was "just a bit of grissle." (Gristle?) But as Skinny said, even if you believe her – which she personally did not – you don't pay out good dinner money just to be given bits of gristle. (I think this is the way it's spelt.) And as I said, it's not very nice to think you're chewing on pieces of dead animal anyway, whether it's pieces of worm or pieces of lamb.

Skinny didn't seem quite so sure about this until I pointed out to her that she wouldn't want to eat Lulu, would she, and she went a bit pale and said no of course she wouldn't. Whereupon I said so where was the difference between eating Lulu and eating a lamb, and she said she thought there was one but she couldn't think what it was.

We talked about it for a bit and in the end she agreed that if she saw a lamb in a field she wouldn't want to go and kill it, and it was only the fact that it came ready wrapped and not looking like a lamb that made her able to eat it. I said, "I bet if someone gave you a whole raw lamb to cook you wouldn't ever eat lamb again," and she really didn't have any arguments left.

So then I said that I was seriously thinking of becoming a vegetarian, and Skinny said that she was, too. I said, "When shall we do it?" and she thought about it a bit and said, "Next term?" I said, "Why next term and not this?" and she said because of Christmas. She said they always have roast turkey at Christmas and she didn't think she could live without roast turkey. Not this Christmas. Maybe next Christmas when her taste buds had changed. (It was me who told her her taste buds would change. I don't know if it is true, but it's what Slimey said to Mum so I hope it is.)

We have agreed, therefore, and made a solemn pact, that next term we shall become veggies. I of course could become one immediately, since we shan't be having roast turkey on account of dead things in the fridge, but it seems better to keep the Skinbag company and start at the same time so that we can encourage each other when our spirits flag or our carnal appetites threaten to get the better of us. Also I don't want Mum crowing. I will tell her the good news after Christmas and not before. This evening it is Hallowe'en and some kids are roaming the streets dressed up as ghouls and ghosts and skeletons. Slimey said, "Don't you go and trick-or-treat?" But that is something I have never done. I don't know why; I just haven't. Skinny doesn't either. Slimey said that next year we must make a Big Thing of it and have fun. He likes to make Big Things of things. On Saturday it is Guy Fawkes night and he is taking me and Mum and Skin to a firework display. I suppose I am quite looking forward to it, really.

Tuesday

I am reading Slimey's book. It is called *I Capture the Castle* by a person with the very strange name of Dodie Smith. What kind of name is Dodie? A strange one! But the book is brilliant. Very funny and yet r-r-r-romantic!

It is all about a girl called Cassandra who wants to be a writer and is keeping a diary, just like me, except that she lives in an old ruined castle and her family don't have very much money, in fact they don't have any money at all on account of her father, who is also a writer, sitting up in the turret reading books all day and not doing any work. It is so cold that Cassandra has to sit on the draining board wrapped up in a blanket with her feet in the sink to write her diary. She has a beautiful older sister called Rose and a weird but equally beautiful stepmother called Topaz, who used to be an artist's model. The romance comes in when two Americans, Neil and Simon, arrive on the scene. Simon is a bit old and has a beard but Neil is gorgeous. This is as far as I have got. I think that probably Rose will marry Simon and that Cassandra, maybe, will fall in love with Neil.

Oh, I nearly forgot. There is also a nice-looking but rather dopey boy called Steven. Steven loves Cassandra and Cassandra is very fond of him but not in the way that he would like. The family owe Steven a great deal as he works for them for nothing and also goes out and earns money which he gives them. Without him they would not survive.

I have never read a book quite like this before and I can't wait to get back to it! I thought after horrors it would be slow and boring but it is not at all. Skinny is going to read it when I have finished.

Thursday

I forgot to write in here yesterday.

Friday

Stewed sewage and gunge. Thank goodness we have decided to go veggie!

Saturday

This morning we went to buy some fish for the pond. Fish, I feel, are basically uninteresting. All they do is swim up and down and gobble with their mouths.

I kept pointing out ones I thought we should have but these, it seems, all the ones I wanted, are warm water fish and not suited to outdoor life. They wouldn't be, would they? Mum said, "Oh, for goodness' sake, Cherry, stop being so awkward! You know perfectly well this is a pond, not an aquarium." I said, "If we'd had an aquarium we could have had some of the pretty ones." At least you could sit and look at them and get a bit of pleasure that way. Mum snapped (she is always snapping these days), "If it weren't for Roly you wouldn't have anything!"

I beg her pardon. If it weren't for Roly I could have my dog.

Now the pool is full of boring old fish that half the time you can't even see. If we had a dog he could get in there and chase them.

I nearly forgot to mention that this evening we all went to the fireworks display. It was up in the park and it was really good. Skinny doesn't like the bangers, but I do! The louder the better is what I say. (Mum and Slimey like the pretty ones. Wouldn't you know it?)

↑
me

↑
Roly

↑
Mum

Sunday

Oh ho ho! Something has eaten the fish. They think it might be a heron. I am sorry for the fish but herons need to eat and if stupid human beings will go digging ponds in their back gardens and filling them with food, what do they expect? They might just as well write a big sign saying:

Mum says I am cruel and heartless but I am not. It is in a heron's nature to eat fish. They are programmed to eat fish. They can't do anything else. It is what the fish expect. And anyway Mum still eats prawns, she says it's her "one weakness". What are prawns if not fish? I told her this and she snapped (again), "That is not the point!"

So if that is not the point, what is?

141 Arethusa Road
London W5

6 November

Dear Carol,

I am too cross to be civil. I am almost too cross to write. Cherry is trying my patience beyond the limits!

Yesterday we stocked the pond with fish and this morning when we woke up almost all of them had gone (a heron, we think). Roly was devastated. He had already begun to personalise them. There was Goldilocks and the Cheeky Chappie and Bright Eyes. Bright Eyes is still with us, but Goldilocks and the Cheeky Chappie have both gone. Two of his favourites! That wretched child thought it was funny. She actually laughed. She made some joke about putting up a sign saying "Breakfast this Way". Then she said, quite rudely, that I still ate prawns so what was I so upset about?

I tell you, I could have hit her! She simply tramples over all Roly's emotions. She is too young to realise what a rare and precious thing it is to find a man who has feelings and isn't afraid of showing them. I suppose she takes it as some kind of weakness and like a typical bully can't resist putting the boot in.

Roly, as usual, speaks up in her defence. He says

that you can't really bond with a fish and that she is quite right, herons have to eat. She could still try to be at least a little sympathetic! Roly has slaved over that pond in an attempt to please her. How far do you have to go to try and keep your children happy?

To the ends of the earth, says Roly, if that is what it takes. We bring them into this world, he says; they do not ask to be born. I retort that he played no part in bringing this particular little horror into the world but he says that he has gatecrashed her living space and hijacked her mother and that she has every right to show her displeasure.

I don't think she has! You couldn't find a better man than Roly.

Lots of love,

Patsy

PS Forgive self-pity and bad manners, I know I'm a rotten correspondent. But Cherry is so trying!

PPS Don't forget I want a photograph!

Monday

I wish I hadn't laughed about his stupid old fish. He spent ages picking them out, choosing the ones with personalities. Well, he said they had personalities. Perhaps he really thinks they do. It is true he wouldn't have had time to get attached to them, I don't think, but I can see that it was a bit upsetting for him. He is quite soft about animals and as a matter of fact so am I, which is why I am glad I have decided after Christmas to give up eating them. Mum is giving up because of Slimey but I am giving up because of principles. Also because of not wishing to be poisoned, but that is really only a small part of it.

I am not sure why Skinny is doing it. Maybe just because of me. She does like animals, but I don't think she truly appreciates how lucky she is to have a dog. Sometimes she grumbles about having to take Lulu for her walks. I would never do that. If I had a dog I would take it out happily and gladly every single day.

my dream

I thought of telling Slimey that I was sorry I laughed about his fish, but if I did Mum would think it was because of her getting mad at me. He would be bound to tell her. They tell each other everything. When I am married I will still want to have secrets. *If* I am married. It might be difficult, living in a cardboard box.

Tuesday

Found out about Parents' Evening and rang Dad. He said, "Right! Got it. It's going in my diary. Have you told your mother?" So I went and told Mum and she wailed, "Oh, Cherry! Did you have to?" I said, "Have to what?" and she said, "Invite your father!" I said, "It is *Parents' Evening*." And Dad is my parent.

There wasn't very much she could say to that.

I know why she doesn't want him there. It's because she wants to drag Slimey along with us. Well, it's *my* school and Dad's *my* parent and he's going to come whether Mum likes it or not!

Wednesday

Told Skinny about Dad coming to Parents' Evening. She said, "What about Roly?" I said, "What about him? He's not my dad!" Skinny said she knew that, but wouldn't he be hurt?

Why should he be hurt? He can go to Bernard Butter's rotten Parents' Evening. He's not coming to mine!

Friday

Forgot to write in here yesterday. I keep forgetting to write. I forgot last week, as well, only then it was Wednesday. And all I wrote on Thursday was just one line. Partly this is because of the enormous gigantic amount of homework they give us at this school and partly it is because of having to stay late for rehearsals and partly it is because of wanting to get back to my book. The *I Capture the Castle* book. I am nearly at the end of it and am getting worried about what is going to happen. I couldn't bear it if Rose got Neil!

Saturday

She did! She got him! And Cassandra ended up with boring old Simon. If it hadn't been for that it would have been one of the very best books I have ever read. Well, it still is one of the best books I have read but I think she got the ending wrong, that is all. I am going to write a note to Slimey and tell him so. And then I am going to put the note under the door of the back room where he does his elves.

I have written the note. It is a nice one to make up for laughing about his fish.

What I have said is this:

Dear Roly,
I have read I Capture the Castle by Dodie Smith and I think if she had got the ending right it would have been an extremely good book. Unfortunately she got it wrong by letting Rose go off with Neil and leaving Cassandra with Simon who is too old and boring and has a beard. Apart from that I thought it was a very good and interesting book which I enjoyed reading. Now I am going to lend it to my friend the Melon and see what she thinks. But I think she will agree with me about Simon.
xxx Cherry.

I put the xxx bit just to be polite.

Sunday

Sereena came over for tea. It was Mum's idea. I kept waiting eagerly for her to start telling some of her dirty jokes but she just sat there looking like she's made of marshmallow, all soft and sweet and gooey.

Marshmallow Sereena

Double YUCK!

It was repulsive! Specially as I happen to know what she's really like. I told her about Slimey's book that he gave me and she said it sounded as though it would be a bit too grown-up for her. How two-faced can you get? She said, "I'm still reading Judy Blume." "Oh, you mean like *Forever*?" I said, kicking at her ankle underneath the table. Her satellite dishes went huge as flying saucers. She said, "That's a rude one, isn't it? My mum wouldn't like it if I read that."

Mum said, "Three cheers for your mum!" which was a totally meaningless remark considering she hasn't the faintest idea what *Forever* is about. At least, I don't think she has. It was also hypocritical, since she has never stopped me reading anything I wanted. She was just sucking up to Sereena.

I was really disappointed in that girl. Talk about playacting! Now of course Mum is convinced she's the sweetest thing there ever was and is trying to talk Mrs Swaddle into sending her to Ruskin Manor next term. She thinks she would be a good influence on me. Ha!

13 November

Dear Carol,

Things go from bad to worse. Now she won't even talk to Roly but simply puts notes under his door! Well, one note. Ungracious as usual. She says she liked *I Capture the Castle* but thought the ending was wrong. She says Cassandra should have had Neil, as Simon is too old and has a beard. I pointed out rather tartly that as a matter of fact, if she had read the book properly, she would have noticed that he shaved it off, but she said she had read it properly and she knows he shaved it off but it didn't make any difference, she still thought of him as having a beard. She said that he was "a beardy sort of person" and that Rose going off with Neil ruined the entire story. How perverse can you get?

Roly says she is simply exercising her critical faculty. He also says that her note is in return for his cards and it shows she is willing at last to start a dialogue. Some dialogue! Ungrateful little beast.

The little girl over the road came to tea this afternoon. Sereena. I personally find her quite delightful – quite refreshingly innocent – and would be only too happy if she and Cherry became friends but Cherry is being her usual churlish self. Whenever I mention her name she either sniggers, as if I've said something secretly amusing, or else she rolls her eyes and groans, as if I've said something incredibly moronic. Roly, surprisingly enough, has not taken to her. Sereena, I mean. He said there is something that doesn't quite ring true but he cannot put his finger on it. I told him that he has lived with my ghastly daughter for too long and has forgotten what normal, nice children are like!

Who'd be a mother? Tell your gorgeous Hunk that you intend to preserve your sanity and remain childless!

All my love,

Patsy

Monday

When I got home from school today there was a parcel waiting for me from America! I tore it open and inside was a box which said "Armadillo Droppings" with a picture of an armadillo. An armadillo looks like this:

Armadillo droppings look like this:

They are round and squidgy and treacle-coloured and you can eat them! Of course they are toffees in fact, but very realistic. Mum said, "Trust Texans!" and shuddered when I offered her one. She said, "They'll stick your teeth up." Slimey on the other hand ate two and said they were "yummy" (which is the sort of word he likes to use). For once I have to agree with him! They are incredibly, scrumptiously yummy! I ate four, one after another, until Mum told me to stop being piglike, which is unfair to pigs who are actually not greedy animals left to themselves, but anyway I thought I had better stop or I would have eaten them all and I want to take them in to school tomorrow and see people's faces when I say, "Have an armadillo turd!"

Now I suppose I must write and say thank you. It is much easier to pick up the telephone, even all the way to Texas, but Mum would have a fit so I'd better not.

Tuesday

I took the armadillo droppings to school and everyone thought it was hilarious except for Mrs James who said, "What on earth have you got there, Cherry?" and when I showed her she pulled a face and said, "That is what I call bad taste." I don't call it bad taste! I call it scrummy! She should have tried one, but she wouldn't. Some people just have no sense of humour.

I went over to Sereena's place when I got in from school

and showed her the box (which now alas was empty). I waited till we were in her bedroom as I didn't think her mother would like it. All Sereena said was, "I bet they didn't look anything like the real thing!" I said, "They did. They looked just like it." She said, "How do you know? Have you ever seen an armadillo dropping?" I had to admit that I hadn't. Then she told me something really gross.

She told me that the brother of her best friend Sharon where she used to live works as a camera man for a TV crew and one day they went into this prison to make a film and they wanted to show the prisoners emptying their buckets that they'd done things into during the night and she said, "They didn't want to use the real thing 'cos that would be horrid and smelly so they made up this yellow mixture with lemonade powder and then they got some brown *playdo* and rolled it in porridge oats and dropped it into the lemonade water with bits of toilet paper and you couldn't tell the difference." She said, "That's the sort of thing they do when they make films."

Ugh! I think that's far nastier than armadillo droppings. And that was in *England*.

Wednesday

When I got in from school Mum told me that there had been a telephone call from Dad saying that unfortunately he wouldn't be able to get to Parents' Evening after all as he had a meeting to attend and wouldn't be finished in time. Mum said, "I'm sorry, sweetheart. I know you really wanted him to come."

It isn't very often that Mum calls me things like sweetheart. I knew it was because she was feeling sorry for me, and not wanting to gloat (on account of she'd said all along that Dad wouldn't turn up, or if he did it would only be to annoy her).

"It is quite a long way for him to travel," she said, trying, I suppose, to make things seem better.

I said, "He promised!" But what do grown-ups' promises mean? Mum promised me a dog, Dad promised to come to Parents' Evening. Neither of them did what they said.

I tried ringing Skinny Melon, thinking it would be nice to have a bit of a laugh about something – anything, really – but all the Melon wanted to do was moan about our maths homework which she said she couldn't understand. If the Melon can't understand it I certainly won't be able to. I'm not going to bother with it. Why should I?

Thursday

Tomorrow is Parents' Evening, which a few days ago I was looking forward to. Now I just think it's a drag. Last year when I was at Juniors, Mum went on her own.

This year she's making me go with her. She's also taking Slime, which is what she wanted all along.

I said, "Why do I have to come?" She said, "Because you're the one it's all about." So then I said, "Why does he have to come?" and she said, "If you're referring to Roly, it's because he's just as interested in your welfare as I am." Then she added, "Though sometimes I wonder why he bothers."

I haven't asked him to bother. I don't want him to come. Trying to get round me, Mum said, "Surely it will be nicer for you to have both of us there?" I said, "Why?" And she said, "Well, it's more normal to have two parents, isn't it?" I said, "Not really. Not these days. There's lots of kids with only one." To which she snapped, "So what have you been making all the fuss about?"

What fuss? I never made any fuss.

She said, "If there are all these other kids whose parents have got divorced, what's so special about you?"

I never said there was anything special. And just because I'm not the only one whose mum and dad have split up doesn't make it any better. It's my dad I care about.

I didn't say any of this to Mum. We don't ever really talk about things like that. We just get mad at each other and she snaps and tells me I'm selfish and ungracious, which is what she did now.

It's true I was in quite a bad mood tonight. I don't know why. Sometimes I just am.

Friday

As we were about to set off for school to go to Parents' Evening, Slimey suddenly said, "Cherry, do you mind me coming along? I won't if you'd rather I didn't."

It made me feel terrible. He'd got dressed up specially in his best clothes. He looks all funny and peculiar in them, like a sort of long floppy beanstalk inside a suit. His trousers bag at the back because he hasn't got any bum and his pockets sag because he keeps things in them. Pens and pencils and little notebooks for drawing. I wanted to say that as far as I was concerned I'd rather he didn't come anywhere near the place, but I couldn't bring myself. I just mumbled something like, "That's all right, I don't mind." His face went into this big happy beam and that was that. I was stuck with him. It wouldn't have been so bad if they hadn't looked so odd, but what with Mum being all fat with the baby and Slimey being all bean-stalky and thin, they made a right weird couple.

We were the *only people* who didn't turn up in a car. At least, I should think we were. Amanda Miles said to me the other day, "Can't your dad afford a car?" I don't know how she knew he hadn't got one, but anyway as I pointed out he's not my dad. And as I also pointed out, he could probably afford half a dozen cars if he wanted them. The number of elves he draws, he ought to be able to. I said, "It's a matter of principle. He happens to care about this earth and the creatures that live on it." She said, "What are you talking about?" I said, "Pollution. Cars ought to be done away with," and she said, "Oh, that's just nutty!"

I used to think it was but now I'm not so sure. Slimey pointed out the other day that all the fir trees up and down our road have gone brown and died. All of them. Mum says maybe it's a tree disease, but Slimey and I think it's acid rain.

Parents' Evening was quite embarrassing, actually. I knew it would be. I had to stand there while Mum and Slimey slunk about talking to all the teachers and I could just feel that people like Amanda Miles were looking at Slimey and sniggering. And then old Slimey keeps making these pathetic jokes all the time and some of the teachers are polite and pretend to think it's funny while some of them – Miss Milsom, for instance, she's really sour – just pinch their lips together and make their nostrils go all thin and you can tell they're thinking, "What an idiot!"

As a matter of fact I felt a bit sorry for him. I mean, he's completely ludicrous-looking, with his silly scraggly beard and this huge Adam's apple that keeps bobbing up and down every time he swallows and these enormous hands and feet that go clump, clump, clump, everywhere. He's really clumsy. But he does try ever so hard to be liked and I guess it's not his fault he keeps doing it all wrong. He just doesn't know any better. I didn't like the thought of Amanda sniggering at him. I felt like telling her that at least old Slimey doesn't go round eating animals or poisoning the planet with noxious fumes like I bet her dad does. Drawing elves might strike some people as a pretty drippy thing to do but no one can deny that it's harmless. And I suppose if you were only four years old it might bring pleasure to your little infantile life. I expect if I am to be truthful I probably quite liked elves when I was four years old.

Actually as a matter of fact I am not being fair to Slimey. He doesn't only draw elves. He doesn't really draw elves at all. Just in this one particular book that he did for tinies. Mostly what he draws are animals and people. Funny animals and people. Even his elves were funny elves.

I wish I could draw like he can!

↑my elves

Saturday

Sereena wanted to know whether I would go and have tea with her again, but I said I couldn't as I was going swimming with Skinny Melon. Mum got a bit cross when she heard. She said, "Why couldn't Sereena go with you?" It's hard to explain that Skinny and I don't want anyone with us. We are a pair. We like being just us. Mum ought to understand since she seems to like being on her own with Slimey.

I told this to Skinny and she said that Mum probably likes being with Slimey because he makes her laugh. She said, "He's really funny, he ought to be on telly."

Slimey? Maybe there is more to him that I thought!

Dad rang up tonight. He said he was very sorry he hadn't been able to get to Parents' Evening. "But you know how it is… meetings that go on for ever." I said that it was all right. I added that he hadn't really missed much. He said, "No, but I do feel bad about it."

I was going to suggest that maybe he could come to the school play instead, and hear me sing, but before I could do so he was called away by Rosemary. I could hear her voice yelling at him up the hall. "Gregg, are you coming?" Dad said, "Oops, got to go! I'll ring you back tomorrow."

I have decided that I hate Rosemary.

Sunday

Wonders will never cease! Slimey has shaved off his beard!!! Unfortunately he looks even more peculiar without it. He has these rabbit teeth and not very much chin.

Spot the difference

Oh, what does Mum see in him?

I know what she sees in him. It is what Skinny says; she thinks he is funny. And also he doesn't keep shouting or losing his temper. I have never heard him shout. He has quite a quiet sort of voice altogether, really. And he does these silly nice things like the other day for instance when we were walking up the road and he saw this worm in the middle of the pavement. Instantly he stopped and broke a bit of twig off someone's hedge so that he could pick it up and put it in a garden. He said it would dry out if it were left where it was.

There aren't many people that would care about a mere worm. I wouldn't have done before. Dad used to go into the back garden and tread on snails. Not purposely, but simply because they happened to be there and got in his way. Slimey never does that. He steps over them. Whenever you go into the garden early in the morning he says, "Watch out for snails!" It used to madden me but I've kind of got used to it. I suppose you can get used to most things.

The only thing I will never get used to is Mum breaking her promise about my dog. How could she do that to me?

20 November

My dear Carol,

So very many thanks for the armadillo droppings (a great success with my crude daughter!) and for the mug-shot of your DHT (Divinely Handsome Texan!) What is he doing working for a bank??? Why isn't he in the movies? On second thoughts, keep him in the bank! He's safer there.

I must tell you that Roly has shaved off his beard. I feel a bit guilty about it. He grew that beard when he was a boy of twenty to cover up the fact that he doesn't have much chin. He doesn't, poor love! And I honestly think he looks far better with a beard. But Cherry hated it – not that she ever actually said so, but she has ways of making her feelings obvious – and as you know he will go to almost any lengths in his efforts to please her.

This all came about, this beard thing, because on Friday it was Parents' Night at Cherry's school and Roly was keen to come along and "be a proper parent" as he put it, but he was scared that Cherry might not want him to. He asked her if she minded and for a wonder she was quite polite and said no, which made Roly really happy, but later that evening, after she was in bed, he suddenly said, "She was ashamed of me, wasn't she?" Of course I indignantly said no – what right has that little miss to be ashamed of a man like Roly? – but nothing would shift his conviction.

He jumped up and went over to the mirror and said, "Look at me! I'm just a mess! If I want her to be proud of having me for a father, I'm going to have to get my act together."

So now he has shaved off his beard and oh, Carol, it is such a mistake! With the beard he looked what he was – an artist. Now he looks like a – a chinless wonder! Only I haven't the heart to tell him. He is absolutely convinced that Cherry will prefer him like this. I don't think I could bear it if she made some hurtful comment. It is truly frightening, the power that children have.

Remember! Stick to your guns with the DHT… you are a career woman!

All my love,

Patsy

Monday

Amanda Miles said to me today, "Was that your stepfather that was with you on Friday?" I couldn't think who she was talking about for a moment as I don't think of Slimey as being my stepfather but I suppose he is. So I said, "Yes. Why?" And she gave this silly smirk and said, "Oh, I just wondered." I felt like hitting her.

Tuesday

Nothing very much happened today.

Wednesday

Nor today.

Thursday

Nothing seems to be happening at all in my life right now.

Friday

Dad never rang me last Sunday, like he promised. Maybe he will this Sunday. If that woman lets him.

Skinny came back with me after school and we watched a DVD but she couldn't stay the night as she has to go and visit her gran over the weekend. She said, "Dire Melvyn's going to drive us there in his posh car." I said, "What's he got? A Merc?" Skinny didn't know. "Something big and shiny," is all she knows. She's useless at things like that.

"I think we ought to go by train," she said. "Otherwise we're polluting the atmosphere."

She picked that up from Slimey. She'd never have thought of it for herself.

Saturday

I don't know how much longer I can go on writing this diary. It is very difficult when one's life is completely empty. I know it is good practice if one day I want to be a writer but if books are still around when I grow up I think I would rather draw the pictures that go inside them than have to write the words. I think actually I am quite good at drawing. This, for instance, is Slimey before and after:

Sunday

It rained all day. Dad still didn't ring.

27 November

Dear Carol,

I just got yours in which you remind me that when we were young and read *I Capture the Castle* we held exactly the same view as Cherry regarding men with beards.

You say, "I couldn't bear the thought of Cassandra being stuck with Simon. To an eleven year old he seemed practically senile!" Yes, you're quite right. One forgets, perhaps, what it is like to be eleven years old.

And I have been thinking, too, about what I wrote last week. That bit where I said what power children wield. They don't, of course, compared with adults. We're the ones who decide their lives for them – what they're going to be called, where they're going to school, where they're going to live – who they're going to live with. It wasn't Cherry's decision that Gregg and I should split up. The only power she's exercising is the power to hit back. I just wish she wouldn't pick on Roly! But children instinctively go for one's weakest spot. She knows very well that by hurting Roly she hurts me.

I'm feeling a bit down at the moment. Beginning to doubt if things will ever come right. Cherry is obviously never going to forgive me for splitting with Gregg and that means she is never going to accept Roly. What a mess!

But life at least is beginning to work for you. You've been through the dark days and come through them. And I don't ever remember you moaning and groaning the way I do!

All love from your wimpish

Patsy

Monday

Asked the Melon if she'd found out what car Dire Melvyn drives and she said she'd forgotten to look. She said she's not interested in his car. She's not interested in him. She wishes her mum had never met him. She is sick and tired of him always being there.

I said I knew how she felt because it was exactly what I'd felt when Mum started going out with Slimey Roland. I thought this was the sort of thing she would like to hear, but all she did was snap at me. She said, "That was totally different!"

How? That is what I should like to know. The Melon is really becoming very grumpy these days.

No card from Slimey for ages. Perhaps he's got the message at last?

Tuesday

I hope Mum hasn't gone and told old Slime that I chuck his cards in the waste-paper basket. It's just the mean sort of thing she'd do. I think I'll go and take them out and put them somewhere she can't see them.

I've taken them out. I've put them in a box under the bed. Now I suppose she'll think that I've stopped being on strike and am going to start tidying the rest of the room.

If that's what she thinks then she is wrong. I have only done it not to hurt Slime's feelings.

Wednesday

Dad rang. He said he's been very "tied up" at the office. He also said that he hasn't forgotten his promise to buy me a computer for Christmas. I expect when I've got used to it I will find it quite interesting. At the moment I'm more into drawing and painting. A big parcel of books arrived for Slimey today. They were all the same book, from his publishers. It is one of his *Freddy the Frog* ones. Freddy the Frog looks like this:

not a very good picture of a frog →

Well, something like that. I can't quite draw it as well as Slimey does, but he's had lots more practice than me. I bet I could if I kept at it.

← *better frogs*

I meant to ask Dad about coming to see me in the school play but I forgot. I don't expect it matters. I don't expect he'd have been able to come. He'd probably have a meeting or be going out to an important dinner party. I do see that it is difficult for him, being so busy and living so far away. Also I don't expect that woman would have let him.

Thursday

Twenty-four days to go until Christmas! I wonder what Mum will buy me?

Friday

I asked Slimey Roland at tea-time whether he was a crusty roll and butter or a soft roll and butter. I thought that was quite a good joke. So did Roly. I mean Slimey. He laughed. Mum didn't. I don't think Mum has much sense of humour. She never appreciates my jokes. She said, "He's a great big softie, as you well know, and you do anything to take advantage!"

She's always accusing me of these things. I don't know what she means.

I've been drawing frogs all day long and can now do them almost as well as Slimey.

Saturday

He pushed another card under my door last night. He is not so bad really, I suppose. It's just that he is not my dad!

Sunday

Today I took out all Slimey's cards and read them, which I never really bothered to do before. Once you get used to it, it is quite easy. At first you have to puzzle a bit but then you learn the symbols, like he always draws a 🐝 for words like he or we. And a 🔑 for not. I'm going to write out what they say and practise doing it myself. It would be fun to write picture messages in Christmas cards!

I'm sorry that dogs and cats make me sneeze. What about a tortoise?

I'm sorry,
I'm sorry!
What about a bird?
Or a fish?
I will dig a pond
if you like.

We can have
goldfish, snails,
bullrushes and
water lilies.
It will be fun!

Please don't
eat us!

159

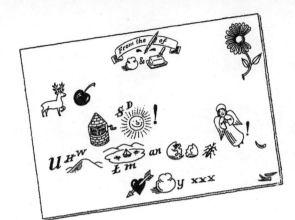

Well done!
You will make
an excellent
angel!

Here are four
examples of
egg jokes.
Exercising,
expelled,
exit, exacting.

eggs-spelled, eggs-it, eggs-acting

Silly, aren't they?

If Sunday is
nice maybe
we'll go for
a picnic.

That was an
ace picnic!
Shall we do it
again some day?
Please look after
Mum when
I'm away.

It's ace to be back!
I miss you and Mum
when I'm not here.

PS Here is
something for
you. I hope you
like her!

Did you like
Snow White?
I did!
Can you say who
all these are?

I hope you are
happy about the
baby? I'm very
happy! I think
a baby will
be fun!

Have you read a book
called "I Capture the
Castle"? It's good.
Take it with you to
read on holiday.

Welcome home!
Good to have you
back. We miss
you when you
are not here.

It's good to have
a pond. Foxes,
badgers and
hedgehogs can
drink there
and it might bring
frogs and toads.

I'm happy that
you like the
book but sad
you didn't like
poor Simon
and his beard.
Maybe he
looked OK
when he
shaved it off?

I hope you like
me better now
that I have no
beard!

I'm crusty when I'm cross and soft when I'm not cross. Today I'm not cross. Today I'm happy! It will soon be Christmas!

I have just realised what the little symbols are down the sides.

She loves me,
she loves me not…
And he always does these
little pictures of a flower.

There aren't many petals left now. I wonder what he'll do when he gets to the end???

I'm not sure yet that I love him, but he's not as bad as I used to think.

Monday

Tuesday

Today we had cowpats and cardboard slices for dinner. Well, that is what I had. Skinny Melon had what looked like armadillo droppings in greasy washing-up water. We both suffered stomach pains, dizziness and a feeling of total norseea. Norsea?

I have not been recording school meals just lately. This is not because they have been good, but simply because I have had too many other things to think about. Like, for instance, the end of term play! Old Roland the Rat and Mum are both going to come, though Mum says she is thinking of bringing ear plugs in case my loud untuneful voice frightens the baby, which she says it well could, even though it is still in the woom. I told her it will give it a feeling for music but Mum only laughed. Mum is very rude about my singing. All I can say is, she is in for a Big Surprise!

One of the seniors who is in the play, called Davina Walters, stayed for an angel rehearsal the other day. When I had finished my solo she cried, "That's it, Cherry baby! Sock it to 'em!" And Miss Burgess told Amanda, who is another angel, that she ought to "take a leaf out of Cherry's book". She said, "Her voice may not always be quite in tune but at least it can be heard."

She only said about it not being in tune because she didn't want to make Amanda jealous. Amanda has a voice like a sick cow.

I have given up the idea of asking Dad to come. If he said yes and then at the last minute found he was too busy I would be disappointed and hurt so I think it is best not to raise false hopes.

Wednesday

I looked those words up. It is nausea and womb. Why is womb pronounced woom and comb pronounced coam?

I sent a picture message to Skinny Melon in class today and now we are going to do it all the time but not with Mrs James or Miss Milsom as they can be mean.

Thursday

Green grollies in sicky sauce. Yeeeurgh!

Friday

Horse dropping tart. I just don't believe they were mushrooms. They were brown. Whoever heard of brown mushrooms?

Dad just rang! He said, "I haven't got anything special to talk about but I thought I'd call and say hello and find out how you're getting on." I said I was getting on OK except for maths and computers and CDT and also home ec. where Mrs Marshall despairs of me. I know this for a fact because she said so. She said, "Cherry Waterton, I despair of you." This was because I sewed a hem all wrong and she had to unpick it and start again, and when she gave it back to me I said, "I'm left-handed, does it matter?" And of course it did because I sew from a different direction.

I told this to Dad and he laughed and said, "All the best people are left-handed." I wonder if this is true? I have just realised that old Ratty is, though I didn't say this to Dad.

So anyway we talked for a bit and then Dad said he had to go but that we must "see each other again very soon", so before I could stop myself I said why didn't he come to the school play and hear me sing, but he said unfortunately he couldn't do that as he is so busy. All these Americans keep coming over and Dad is the only person who can deal with them.

At least it is better to know now than to think he is coming and then he doesn't.

Saturday

Went shopping with Mum and Roland Rat and saw brown mushrooms! I never noticed them before. But the ones they dished up at school were all soft and squashy so I still think they were horse droppings. I expect they get them cheap by the bucketful.

Sunday

Sereena came over and I taught her how to do picture messages. That girl has a mind like a sewer. All she could think to do was giggle and draw pictures of lavatories and bums.

That's have and bump. Geddit? Roly Rat is far cleverer than that.

What he would do is:

But Roly is a real artist. Sereena is just stupid. She has a one-track mind. Also she said something which annoyed me so much that I shouted at her. I was showing her some of Roly's picture messages and she said that personally she thought they were somewhat childish. I snapped, "Oh do you? Well, for your information that is just where you're wrong. My stepdad happens to be a totally brilliant picture book artist who has had books published in every country in the world. Even in Russia. Even in Japan."

That shut her up.

Monday

I told the Skinbag about Sereena and Skin said that she sounded like a very obnoxious kind of person. I said that she is and that I hoped now I had snubbed her she would stay away from me. I think she had some nerve saying that about poor old Roly Rat's drawings. The Melon agrees. She thinks Roly is the cat's whiskers. She said today that she wished her mum could meet someone like him.

Tuesday

Only 12 days to go till Christmas! Mum asked me this evening what I wanted as my Christmas present and I said, "You know what I want! I want a dog." She sighed and said, "Oh, Cherry, we've been into all this! Roly can't help being allergic. Don't be so selfish all the time."

I don't call it selfish wanting someone to keep their promise that they made you. I said, "If I can't have what I want then I don't want anything," which Mum said was just cutting off my nose to spite my face. Whatever that is supposed to mean.

nose →

I think what it means is that I'm not going to get a dog anyway, so I might as well accept it and find something else. But I can't think of anything else! Not anything big. I told Mum this and she said that I must be a very contented person to have so few wants. I would be contented, if I could have my dog. I would even be contented living with Slime.

Wednesday

11 days! I am marking them off on the calendar. It is a pity the baby is going to miss Christmas. February seems a long time to wait.

Thursday

10 days!

We had the dress rehearsal for the play this afternoon, which meant we were let off lessons, hooray! I hate Thursday afternoons as it is double maths and Mr Fisher says I am the only person he knows who can take one away from two and make it come to three. I said that was because I am a naturally creative person and he told me not to be cheeky but his eyes sort of crinkled as he said it so I don't think he will report me.

The dress rehearsal went really well. At least, it did for me. Amanda Miles and some of the others forgot their words and had to be prompted, but I was word perfect. A few of the teachers came and sat at the back of the hall and watched and at the end, one of them I don't know said, "I like the angels." Miss Burgess said, "Could you hear them all right?" And he said, "All except the little redhead," (meaning Amanda, who is carroty) and then he pointed at me and said, "The police could use that one as a siren." Miss Burgess said, "Oh, yes, we never have any problems with Cherry." Amanda hated me for it, you could tell.

Friday

Last night old Roly Rat pushed another card under my door. It was quite a nice one, he made it look like a telegram, so I took it to school with me and stuck it on the wall of our dressing room (which is only one of the classrooms by the side of the hall). Everyone wanted to know what it said, so I translated it for them and they all thought it was really good except for Amanda who said she'd sooner have a proper telegram, but nobody agreed with her.

Miss Burgess told me that I ought to keep it as it might be valuable one day. She said, "It's an original drawing, and your stepfather is quite famous."

Is he? I never thought of Roly Rat as being famous! I didn't tell Miss Burgess I had a whole stack of his drawings at home. But I'm glad now that they weren't thrown out with the rubbish, which is what would have happened if I hadn't gone on strike. Mum would simply have emptied my waste-paper basket into the dustbin. I like Ratty's cards and I'm going to keep them to show my own children, if I ever have any (if I am not living in a cardboard box). Not because they might be valuable but because they are funny and interesting.

My performance tonight was quite good I think. At the end all the angels had to go in front of the curtain to be clapped and afterwards I was taken home by Skinny Melon's mum and her boyfriend, Dire Melvyn, in Dire Melvyn's car (which is a BMW! Dead posh), as Mum and Ratty are not coming until tomorrow. Dire Melvyn said, "Well, at least we had no trouble hearing you." and her mum told me that I was a very confident performer. Skinny giggled and said, "She was the Foghorn Angel!" but I don't mind Skinny giggling as she doesn't do it nastily.

I didn't want Mum and Roly Rat coming to the first night in case I had stage fright, but they will be there tomorrow. They are looking forward to it.

Saturday

I was even better tonight! I felt I was really getting into it. I am thinking again about maybe becoming a singer. I know I have the voice for it because that is what everyone says. A vicar came up to me afterwards and said, "Aha! The Angel of the Clarion Call!" Even Mum was impressed, I could tell. And a man from the local paper came to take our photograph and he took one of the angels, and he said, "Where's the little one with the big voice? (Meaning me.) "Let's have her in the middle." Amanda was cross as crabs! She really fancies herself.

Instead of waiting for a bus we all went home by taxi because Ratty said, "It's the only way for a star to travel." Mum said, "Well! I suppose we shall have to pay to speak to you now."

This is us being photographed

Monday

Skinny came to school this morning looking dead miserable. I asked her what the matter was and she said, "Nothing." So then I said, "What did you do on Sunday?" and she said, "Nothing." I said, "I didn't do anything, either. We could have got together if I'd known. But I thought you were going out with Dire Melvyn?" She said, "We did." I said, "So how can you say that you did nothing? You must have done something. Even if you just drove somewhere, that's doing something. You can't call driving somewhere not doing anything. Unless you mean you were just sitting there in a great useless lump suffering from brain death. Maybe that's what you mean?"

She was in a very strange mood. She told me in decidedly huffish tones to just shut up and stop getting on her nerves. Then she didn't speak to me again until break.

Weird. She is all right now, though.

Tuesday

Hooray! We have broken up. Mrs James said our reports will arrive after Christmas. I am not sure whether this is a good thing or a bad thing. Skinny says it's bad as they will be hanging over us but on the other hand it avoids any unpleasantness before Christmas. I expect mine will be foul. Skinny expects hers will be foul too though I don't know why as Skinny on the whole is very quiet and well behaved. I am the one who is always getting told off.

Tomorrow we are going to go out together and buy our presents, both for each other and for other people. We have a rule that we will spend £5 on each other and no more. I think this is a good rule as it stops one from worrying. For instance, if I only bought Skinny a calendar with pictures of dogs (which is what I'm going to do) and she bought me a new pair of Doc Marten's, then I would feel mean and guilty. Not that she is very likely to buy me a new pair of Doc Marten's as she wants a pair herself.

Wednesday

I have bought:

A calendar for Skinny Melon, some leggings for Mum, some aftershave from the Body Shop for Roly Rat and a teddy bear for the baby.

It was very difficult knowing what to get for Roly Rat but in the end I thought if I got something from the Body Shop it would demonstrate that I care about the environment and about things not being tested on animals. That will please him.

I bought the leggings for Mum because I am tired of seeing her in those horrible dungaree things and think it will be good for her to wear something bright and pretty when she no longer has the baby inside her and is back to normal. They are a lovely orange colour with swirly patterns in yellow and purple. She will look really great in them. She has nice legs when they are not hidden in dungarees.

I bought something for the baby because although I know it is not going to be here until February I think it should have some presents waiting for it. I thought that a bear would be suitable. There were all different coloured ones, pink ones, yellow ones, blue ones, browny ones, so in the end I got a browny one as we don't know whether the baby is going to be a boy or a girl.

I have been wondering which I would rather have, a brother or a sister, and I think on the whole I would rather have a brother as it would be something different. I am quite looking forward to it, I suppose, now that I have got used to the idea. Skinny wants to come and look at it when it's born. She says that she likes babies. I can't imagine why, since as far as I can see they don't actually do anything except eat and sleep. Well, they also mess their nappies and sick up their milk and cry a lot and sometimes scream. They also dribble. All of which I think is pretty revolting.

Skinny says this just goes to show how little I know about them. She says that all these things may be true but that when they are not messing or dribbling or sicking things up they are nice and cuddly and what she calls "fun". She says as well that it is very exciting when they give their first smile and say their first word and grow their first teeth. Hm! We shall see.

Thursday

Today the Skinbag came round and stayed for tea. I asked her if she would like to watch a DVD of Laurel and Hardy which belongs to Ratty, who has dozens of them, and she said all right so I put it on and it was really funny. I was giving myself a pain from laughing so much, and all the time the Melon is just sitting there glum and gloomy with a face like a wet washing-rag, until in the end she starts to get on my nerves and I switch the DVD off and snarl, "What's the matter with you? Has your sense of humour gone?" In reply to which she instantly bursts into tears and informs me that life as she has known it is over.

Well! I am completely taken aback because one thing Skinny is not and that is a watering pot (as Mum calls it). So naturally I ask her why life as she has known it is over, and it all comes pouring out, about Dire Melvyn and her mum and how her mum has just broken it to her that they are thinking of getting married.

My immediate instinct is to remark sarcastically on her sudden change of attitude. Funny that when I used to carry on about old Ratty, the Skinbag could think of nothing better to say than how lucky I was and how any dad is better than no dad and how she wished that her mum would get married again. However, because I am her friend I very nobly suppress my instinct and croon in syrupy fashion that I know just how she's feeling as I've been through it all myself.

"It's not the same," she says; "Roly's nice. Anyone would be glad to have Roly for a dad." And then she goes into these really loud sobs and says that nobody in their right mind would want Dire Melvyn.

So while I'm sitting there wondering what to say next, Mum comes in to tell us that tea's ready, and of course she sees the Melon in floods and wants to know what's wrong so I explain the situation and Mum goes all soft and mumsy (she's never like that with me) and puts an arm round the Melon's shoulders and coaxes her out into the kitchen, where Ratty is, and before I know it the Melon's weeping all over Ratty and saying how Dire Melvyn is the pits and life as she has known it is over.

After a bit, when she's finished blubbing and has blown her nose on Ratty's hanky (I wouldn't! It's all covered in paint), Ratty asks her what exactly is so dire about poor old Melv. I say, "There isn't anything dire. He drives a BMW and he gives her money." But the Melon glowers at me and says he's got this big fat belly and grey hairs growing out of his nostrils and hands like damp fungus and he treats her as if she's about six years old. She says it's all right for Matthew (that's her brother); he's hardly ever at home. And it's all right for the Blob (that's her sister) because she's only eight and doesn't seem to mind if she's treated like an infant.

"But I can't stand it!" wails the Melon.

And then old Ratty says something which surprises me. He says, "The poor man's probably terrified of you. You young girls frighten the lives out of us poor, plain middle-aged men." I said, "*Do* we?"

"You'd better believe it!" said Roly.

The Melon hiccuped and said she didn't see any reason why Dire Melvyn should be terrified of her.

"Because he's desperate to make a good impression," said Roly. "He's desperate for you to approve of him and it makes him nervous." And then he told her to try being kind to him and to laugh at his jokes and maybe even ask his advice about something, because that would make him feel that he was wanted. He promised that if she did, it would work miracles.

I could see that the Melon was doubtful, but at least it shut her up and stopped her dripping all over the place. When her mum came to collect her (in her old VW) I went out to the car with her and reminded her, in what I hoped were comforting tones, that when Mum first got married to Roly I thought he was the biggest creep around. "And now," I said, "I quite like him." I said that what happened was, you sort of grew used to them.

The Melon just gave me this dying duck look and clunked her seat belt. She really is making a big production of it. I suppose she wants to be the centre of attention. Pathetic, really. I didn't make anywhere near this amount of fuss.

Incidentally, I have discovered what Mum has bought me for Christmas! It is on top of the wardrobe as usual. She always puts my presents up there. She thinks I don't know but I found out years ago. It is not cheating to look, as it is only the lesser ones. My big ones she hides somewhere else that I have not yet discovered.

I only took a very quick peek. Some of the things are in bags and when they are in bags I don't look. That is one of the rules. But I saw a couple of CDs which I really want, so that is good. There are also what I suspect may be books (flat and hard) and some that I think are clothes (soft when you poke them). That is good, too!

Friday

Horrors! Today I had a fright. I went in with Mum to do some last-minute shopping (Roly Rat stayed behind to draw some last-minute elves) and we walked through the tights and leggings department and Mum suddenly said, "Maybe I shall splash out and buy myself a pair of leggings. What do you think?" and she headed straight for the very pair that I had bought for her! Very quickly I said, "You don't want those. What about these ones?" pointing to some drab and boring ones in plain colours. To my great relief she said, "Yes, I suppose those are rather more suited to a middle-aged woman, aren't they?" It was a tense moment!

I have wrapped up all my presents in Christmas wrapping paper and put little gift tags on them with picture messages.

Roly's says:

Mum's says:

I am going to tidy my room for Christmas.

Saturday

Today I felt the baby move! Mum said, "Oh! He's kicking me." "Or she," I said. "It might be a she." Mum agreed that it might be.

I don't mind which it is. I just want it to get here!

The Melon rang up in the evening to wish me a Happy Christmas. She said that Dire Melvyn was going to be with them for three whole days but that it was "all right" as she had done what Roly said and asked his advice about something. She had asked him what sort of plant she could grow in a really dark and boggy part of the garden (old Skin is quite into gardening), and he had come up with some really brilliant suggestions. It seems he knows about plants and boggy patches, so now she doesn't mind so much about the fungussy hands and grey nose hairs and the big fat belly. What she actually said was, "He's not absolutely as dire as I thought."

Thank goodness for that! It means I can enjoy Christmas without having to worry about her. After all, she is my best friend – my *very* best friend – and I wouldn't have liked to think of her being unhappy.

My dear Carol,

I am writing this on Christmas Eve. Haven't had a chance until now, what with one thing and another.

Last Saturday we went to see Cherry doing her singing angel bit in the school play. Oh, dear! What can one say? They obviously chose her because she looked right – very pretty and cheeky. Very impish. But she cannot sing! Of course we told her she was the greatest, or at any rate Roly did, and as a result she has been blasting our eardrums ever since. I wish she would take up something quiet, such as painting.

Roly has bought her a whole range of pens, paints, crayons, drawing blocks, etc., for Christmas, but as it's from him she'll probably just look at it with that terrible expression of condescension and contempt that girls of eleven can have. Do you know what I mean? Cold and cutting and oh, so knowing and superior! Were we ever like that when we were eleven?

In fairness to her I have to say that she has been quite sweet and considerate these last few days (apart from the ear-blasting). It was very funny the other day!

I was going to splash out and buy myself a pair of leggings and Cherry practically tied herself in knots trying to guide me away from a pair in glaring orange that she has quite obviously bought me for Christmas!!! I shall have to feign utter astonishment when I undo the parcel, just as Cherry will feign utter astonishment when she undoes some of hers. Not very much is a secret in this house. She always climbs up to look on top of the wardrobe because she knows that's where I keep all her "pillow case" presents. She's been doing it for years. It's a sort of game we play, except that she doesn't know that I know she does it! (Don't worry, I have hidden your baseball bat! I spirited it away the minute it arrived.)

I'm a bit worried in case she hasn't bought anything for Roly. I've kept dropping hints but the only kind of hint she understands is the kind that you apply with a sledge-hammer! She is incredibly thick-skinned. So I've got some after-shave from the Body Shop and gift-wrapped it, just to be on the safe side. He would be so terribly hurt if she forgot him.

Meanwhile, we have a real surprise for her! I won't tell you what it is. See if you can guess!

A few weeks ago, in the middle of the night, Roly suddenly shot bolt upright in bed and cried, "I've got it!" When I asked him, "Got what?" he said, "The solution... I'm allergic to fur, not skin. We'll get her a hairless one!"

So we hunted high and low – and incidentally, paid

the earth, though Roly assures me it will be worth it for the pleasure it will bring – and all I will say is that it is HAIRLESS, that it comes originally from CHINA, and that right at this moment it is over the road being looked after by Mrs Swaddle (the mother of Sereena).

Have you guessed???

Roly is going to go over and collect it tomorrow immediately before breakfast. I can't wait to see Cherry's face!

Gregg, incidentally, has kept his word for once and sent her the computer, it was delivered last week while she was at school. I'm sure it will come in very useful but I can tell you here and now that between a hairless Chinese wotnot and a computer there will be no competition!

I do hope you and your Dwayn have the most wonderful Christmas ever. If I could only rid myself of fears that a) Cherry will have forgotten to buy something for Roly and that b) she is going to resent the baby, I would be the happiest soul on earth! I will keep my fingers crossed. Maybe I am misjudging her.

All my fondest love,

Patsy

This is Charlie Chan. He is 4 U.
When he grows up he will look like this

U B him!

and Mum
xxx

xxx

she
loves
you!

Christmas Day

Dear Roly,

Charlie Chan is the best present I've ever had. He makes me very happy. I adore him already! Thank you, thank you, thank you!

Love Cherry XXX

Boxing Day

Now that I have my beautiful Charlie, I won't be keeping this diary any more. I'll be far too busy, taking him for walks! So this is where I am going to end. It has been quite fun and it has done what Mrs James said it would do, it has cleaned out the cupboard, but I feel that from now on I am going to be concentrating more on drawing than on writing. I have decided... when I am grown up I am going to be an <u>artist!</u>

More fantastic reads from Jean Ure:

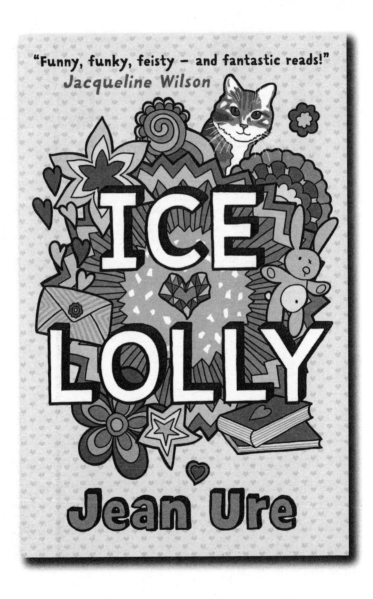

"Funny, funky, feisty — and fantastic reads!"
Jacqueline Wilson

ICE
LOLLY

Jean Ure

Meet frankly fantastic Frankie Foster!

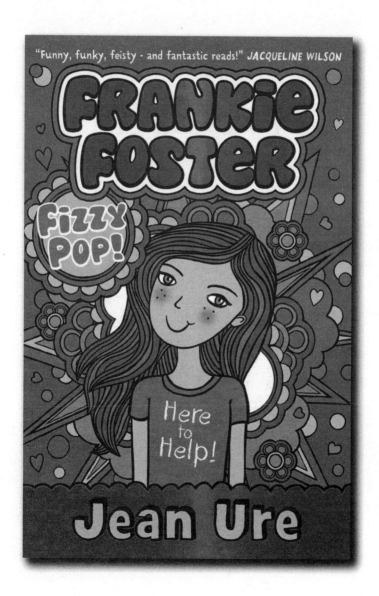

More about Frankie coming soon:

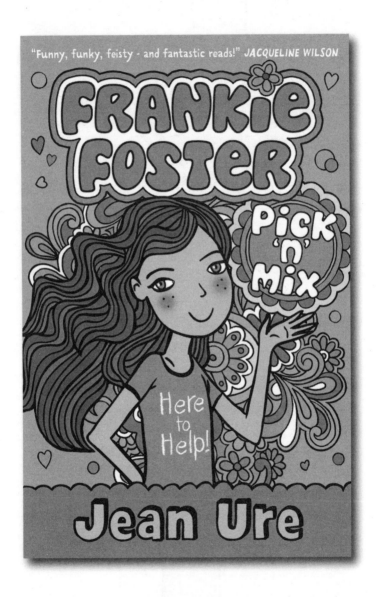

"Funny, funky, feisty - and fantastic reads!" *JACQUELINE WILSON*

FRANKIE FOSTER

Pick 'n' Mix

Here to Help!

Jean Ure